Falling in Love with Bella

by *L. Elaine*

My Dear Friend Al!
Thanks for all the love & support and for always being family! We are blessed you've been in our lives & continue to be with us!
  love,
    l. 10/2019

Acknowledgements

"A man's homeland is wherever he prospers."

~ Aristophanes

Time keeps on moving and yet people want additional stories in this *Dynasty of Love* series—so here we are discovering more about another brother in the Gutiérrez Family—Alberto. It's getting complicated the more I weave the tales of these siblings, their lovers, cousins and friends. So now I've also created a family tree to begin to track the expansion and you can find it at the end of the book, along with the preview of the next book about Cousin Valentino. I hope you enjoy this story as much as you did the previous two books; I certainly enjoyed traveling to these places, doing research and working to make the details come off the page to be imaginable to the reader. Alberto's story was also fun to create: he's devoted to his family and their business, and is taken aback by the arrival of Arabella into the company. More specifically, he's angry the Board gave this woman his prime position of power. A friend asked me why would Arabella leave her only family to travel halfway around the world for a job, and why would the Board take Alberto's position from him to forward corporate progress over family loyalty. See if you can relate to Arabella's desire to make her own way in the world; as well as grapple with what it's like to fight against technology as it changes the way in which we've always done things—do you resist, accept or create a powerful way to live in the midst of circumstances?

During my efforts to finish this book, one of my role models, Toni Morrison, passed away. While it broke my heart to lose a legendary author, I am mindful of a quote she authored, "[i]f there is a book that you want to read, but it hasn't been written yet, you must be the one to write it." That was the push to get it done. Much thanks to so many who supported Alberto and Bella's journey, including those who constantly offered words to sustain me to stay the course and finish this book. While I put finishing an advanced degree in leadership ahead of writing, everyone patiently waited for this publication—thank you, thank you, thank you to my family, friends and fans!

I would be remiss without these additional shout outs: love to my creative children for the artwork and constant patience; continued thanks to Mom, Cousin Jean, Brenda and Andra for being dreamers and enlisting others to get on the *Dynasty of Love* bandwagon; big recognition to my friend Denise for always being there through every line written, and Coach Jen who keeps inspiring me to write the book within so it is given to others; and finally blessings to my great-aunt Lenear, who inspires me to remain vigilant and devoted to family no matter how much time goes by in our lives…

I'll keep writing, if you'll keep reading!

Introduction

"The science of today is the technology of tomorrow."
~ Edward Teller

<u>Falling in Love with Bella</u>, the third book in the *Dynasty of Love* series, takes place mostly in and around Granada and Jaén in the Andalusian region of Spain. This story follows the path of a brilliant scientist, Arabella Mia Gomez, PhD, who leaves her home in America to pursue her scientific and corporate dreams half a world away in Spain. It starts out as a business experiment and quickly turns into a game of passion, love, and honoring family traditions. Shortly after her arrival in Jaén, Arabella realizes she has stepped into more than a family's corporate dynasty, she's taken Alberto Gutiérrez's job as Chief Scientist of Gutiérrez Enterprises. Alberto is the only Gutiérrez brother who still lives at home with his parents and tends to the family estate—and he's none too happy about her new role as his boss. We first mentioned Arabella in book two, <u>Falling in Love with Paradise</u>, and now she gets her very own tale.

The name '*Arabella*' means 'answered prayer.' Long before I started to write this book or even decided on its title, I fell in love with the name Arabella and how it simply exudes beauty. This heroine has spent her life more interested in advance degrees and reading books on chemistry, agriculture, and manufacturing than one's physical beauty. My first thought for the title of this book was *A Fight Worth Losing*! Why? Since college, this heroine has been fighting to have her work not be judged differently because it was produced by a female. That she would dare step into a traditionally male role, expect others to invest in her ideas and be a take no prisoners "nerd," is an opportunity for many of us women to stop apologizing for showing up, speaking up, and continuing to stand up for our right to be in the boardroom. Even in the uncomfortable moments Arabella is still willing to give her heart, and I think that is a beautiful way to be. Hence, I changed this heroine's name from Ariana to Arabella, and the nickname Bella came into existence and a title was formed. Arabella has wild and curly red hair that reminds me of a fierce, fiery personality full of passion and a zest for life! So of course she just had to fall for the one guy who professed he hated her yet secretly desired her—Alberto.

Speaking of Alberto, let me tell you a little bit about him. His personality mirrors the meaning of his name, 'noble and bright.' However, I can't say to you I selected that name for such glorious reasons. Instead, Alberto ended up being one of the "brothers" in this family saga because I once traveled through Spain on a tour, and our amazing guide's name was Alberto. How could I not celebrate that! Now back to Bella's hero: duty, honor and tradition are what makes Alberto tick. He was raised in Jaén like the rest of his brothers. He went away for college, got his education and came back home as a scientist to use what he'd learned to make his family's company a force to be reckoned with in the olive oil industry. He closely watches over his parents, works in the corporate office, the laboratory, on the manufacturing line and also out in the fields. He does it all tirelessly! He is loyal to the traditional ways to harvest the olives and produce the various types of oil that have been in his family for eons. Even though Arabella upsets his way of life and their relationship began with him resenting her place, he still respects her knowledge, innovation and ultimately her position of authority; and surprisingly he works to implement her ideas.

Alberto and Arabella are enemies, until they become passionate lovers. Spending time with each other, they drop their defenses! Real love arises from their working closely together, mutual respect for the other, and willingness to try something new. Go with us on this new adventure as we explore my love of travel from the towns and countryside of Jaén and Granada in Spain, to New York and California and back again to Spain—come watch love blossom and grow into something rare and beautiful...

Chapter 1

"Life affords no higher pleasure than that of surmounting difficulties, passing from one step of success to another, forming new wishes and seeing them gratified." ~ Samuel Johnson

Arabella Mia Gomez turned off the road and drove her late model Honda Civic into the Henderson Winery's parking area. One last stop before she went to the airport to begin her new adventure half a world away in Jaén, Spain.

Here at the winery she would see her brother, Alejandro Samuel Gomez. He was older by four years beyond her thirty-two years of life. And he was all the family she had left after their parents, Alexander and Annmarie, had died years ago. Their parents were both only children of only children. She and Alejandro represented the last generation of relatives unless one of them produced offspring. That was something Arabella was unsure about for herself. Family binds people in ways she could not deny and yet she was in no hurry to create more ties. She rarely thought about having children of her own, and today would be no different.

Alejandro, the rock of her life, was the first one she'd told that she'd been offered the opportunity to go to Spain and implement her olive extraction process on a larger scale. She'd studied agriculture, chemistry and manufacturing in undergraduate and master's programs, graduated top of her class and went on to finish her doctoral work at University of California—Davis. She could've gone into the winemaking business like her parents and brother, but she wanted to focus on a different fruit—olives. After leaving the school's laboratory, she'd spent the last few years perfecting her research on a small scale in some of California's olive oil producing vineyards.

This opportunity in Jaén was her big chance to take her ideas on automation to traditional farms. What better place than Spain, the largest producer of olive oil in the world. As a country, she'd read it was often competing head to head with Italy from year to year to be number one. While olives had been growing in America since the 1800s, it was not nearly as popular as grapes and wine making. Hence, she could escape into her research and ignore being social much more easily.

Olive oil was definitively proven to be good for one's health and diet too. The dichotomy existed that even as healthy as locally grown products would be, most people in the United States were not interested in the American olive oil market. Its share on the mainstream global stage never matched up to Spain and Italy. Perhaps one day the American varieties would dominate a portion of the global space. She suspected that was still a long way off.

Now American wine, specifically labels produced in California, was a different story all together. American consumers preferred California sourced wines over those from foreign shores. No matter the origin, Arabella was a huge fan of drinking wine; it tasted delicious. Everything in moderation of course! She had one rule to follow— do not partake in drinking alone. And she never had, even as tempting as it sometimes was to wallow in a good bottle of vino or to try to forget whatever ailed one's soul.

Right there was her sadness about her parents being gone. Losing them had been a difficult time. They'd died within weeks of each other. True soulmates. Arabella could feel the tears well up. No, no, no! I am not here to think about mom and dad! I am here to begin my new journey!

Working was pretty much all Arabella did on a consistent basis. She didn't really have friends. While growing up, Arabella's mom had labeled the people her daughter knew as "acquaintances," temporary people passing through her life and definitely not worthy of telling one's secrets to. She still often heard those 'acquaintances' say something like "at thirty-two years old, you should have accomplished more, be up to some worthy endeavor other than getting more education and working." She knew what they meant—they thought she should have a husband and family, belong to social or civic organizations, and of course attend happy hour with her girlfriends. They'd go on and on.

Arabella didn't want any of it. She remembered the unsuccessful relationships she'd had while in graduate school; they were a distraction. And rarely did she really align herself with organizations fighting for a cause. All those 'ties' demanded too much of her time. Maybe if a local library needed to be saved, she'd written a letter to government representatives. Or she'd send money to the animal rescue organizations after one of those cry-worthy, late night television commercials she'd watch if she was unable to sleep. Arabella scoffed. Ha, what do my so called 'friends' know? None of them ever seem to be happy anyway. Being on the periphery is good enough and I am content.

Truth be told, Arabella was happiest when working. She had a lot of pent up energy and drive to succeed. Interactions with people were awkward. Expectations and agendas never seemed to be as straightforward as algorithms and formulas. She loved talking to herself in the laboratory or discussing technical terms and philosophies with the research assistants. When free, she swam laps at the campus pool. Her brother said she was a nerd through and through, and she thought it the best name he'd ever called her! She identified with being "nerdy." People usually left her alone. That provided her with reason enough to keep working.

Alejandro told her that he was excited Gutiérrez Enterprises had acknowledged her applied research and its potential benefits for the industry. All that being said, in his next breath he also requested she turn it down, boost her resume and instead approach some of the larger California companies. She wasn't surprised with all seriousness when he requested she "also think it through before uprooting her life for an experiment in Spain." Arabella knew her brother well—always the practical one! He didn't support her leaving California only because he did not want her to be so far away from him. She'd argued she wouldn't be gone forever. He'd countered by reminding her of their promise to always be close. She still remembered his exact words "it's not possible to keep our promise to each other with you on another continent."

She'd laughed noting that physical distance would change nothing about their relationship. They'd been inseparable best buddies all these years. She idolized her brother and answered his phone calls every time, no matter what she was doing, where she was or whom she was with. So what instead of thirty miles of distance separating them, they'd be six thousand miles apart! Technology was on their side after all—with the internet, video calls, email, and new apps being created daily. Worst case, she was at most only a plane ride or two away!

Here she was parked in a visitor's space at the vineyard where she'd grown up, trying to convince herself she could really do this. Since she'd accepted the position, she'd been torn with staying or going. Her mind was now set! There were no guarantees in life. All she owned except her clothes was packed away in storage, a place for her practical car secured, and her research work in California now complete. One conversation left to have! Yes, she would not deny this was going to be an emotional visit with Alejandro, but she would not put her life on hold anymore for comfort and safety. She could always come home. He'd get used to her being away and he could come visit her in Spain too. Hell, if he actually ventured across the Pond, they could meet up in any European city for a short reunion. She'd play tour guide, do all the research and let him boss her around the whole time.

Arabella sighed as she reached over to pick up her identification badge and wallet. This 'goodbye for now' will go fine or so I hope, she whispered as she got out of her car. Head held high, she walked across the lot and into the lobby of the short four story building. Just inside, she saw the security guard and one of the receptionists. "Hi Adam! Hi Kimberly."

"Hi Dr. Gomez," they both said in unison as she flashed her credentials and then put it on the access gate. The gate swung open.

"Going up to see Alejandro, and please stop calling me Dr. Gomez," she said with a smile that was difficult to keep plastered in place. She could feel her emotions welling up inside her chest again. Everyone at the winery had called her 'Lil Bella' her entire life until she'd finished her doctoral degree. While she was no longer little, and didn't come to visit very often anymore, she liked being called Bella instead. This place was home.

"Of course! Alejandro is in the building." Kimberly said smiling as she nodded her assent after looking down at the locator board.

Once on the other side of the gate, Arabella paused to lean against the reception desk where Kimberly was seated. She'd loved hanging around the giant desk for as long as she could remember. "Yeah, Alejandro said stop by before I leave for Spain."

"Ladies, please excuse me, I have rounds to make," Adam said as he strolled away. He turned back around and added, "Bella, all the best!"

"Bye Adam!"

Kimberly's smile widened as she turned her attention to Bella. "Alejandro did mention Lil Bella was off to new groves to his dismay."

"Yes, Big Bro forgot I am way grown and I know how to take care of myself."

"Yes you are all grown up now. Your parents would have said go for it! We are proud of you Bella and I am personally excited for what's possible! You will be great so go knock 'em dead!"

"Thanks Kimberly! I appreciate your support."

"Your brother will come around too. He has always been your protector. Give him some time to get used to you going away."

Arabella squished her face up in a pensive thought. "Yes he will come around. I needed to hear the reminder."

"You're welcome. If you ever need anything, you know how to find me." Kimberly said perkily.

"Yes I do and thanks again for believing in me." She did know how to find Kimberly. They'd grown up together at the winery and her parents had been good friends to Kimberly's parents. Kimberly had been kind to her and Alejandro, especially after her parents' death. She was closer in age to Alejandro than her, yet she was someone who Arabella considered a friend.

Kimberly put her hand on top of Arabella's hand, the one that had been resting on the desk. The gesture pulled Arabella from her thoughts and immediately she realized she'd not been listening. "I'm sorry Kimberly. I was thinking to myself, momentarily distracted." Arabella looked into the woman's smiling eyes. "What were you saying?"

"No worries, it happens. My point is no matter what, we all believe in you Bella, including Alejandro. If your stubborn brother doesn't want to admit it, it's because he's going to miss you more than anyone."

Arabella pondered her friend's words. She could feel real tears threatening to spill from her eyes. She was glad Kimberly had stopped being so formal. This woman was like family. And she needed to get her goodbye with Alejandro over with. She lifted her leaning frame from the desk, turned to fully face Kimberly and gently extracted her hand. "Thanks Kimberly. Now, please don't make me cry even before I see him." She sniffled a little and saw emotion in Kimberly's eyes too. Nooooooo. "Look Kimberly, I have to go now. Take care!"

With that she turned and bounded across the lobby to the elevators. Kimberly said nothing more and Arabella did not turn back around. She made a mental note to leave through the vineyard to avoid saying more goodbyes.

******

Arabella pressed the up button and watched the elevator doors closest to her swing apart. She got on and pressed the number four, instinctively knowing the way to her brother's office. He occupied a corner space on the fourth floor overlooking the vineyards. Memories always flooded in when she walked through the doors of this place. She'd run through these very hallways as a little girl, and grown up as part of the Henderson family. Her parents had met here at the winery and fallen in love. Such a romantic tale. They'd often shared their stories of love, wine and courtship. Arabella never got tired of hearing it.

In the background she heard the elevator doors open. No time to reminisce now, she sighed. Stepping off, she walked into the bright light of sunshine that painted a picturesque scene emanating from the windows. Rows and rows of grape vines and lush hills of greenery for as far as the eyes could see. It was breathtakingly beautiful.

Arabella moved down the corridor and turned the corner to the right. Here we are at my big brother's office. Door closed, she stepped to it and lifted her right hand to knock, resting her hand against the autumn-colored wood. One more steadying breath. She inhaled and slowly exhaled to the count of four, 1-2-3-4. "You can do this!" she said as she knocked on that door. From the other side she could hear him say "Come in!"

Arabella placed her hand on the doorknob, willing it be locked and she was dismayed when it turned and opened. Just inside, more sunshine danced on the rug as it shined through the floor-to-ceiling windows. Tentatively Arabella lifted her eyes to see her brother curiously staring back at her. Silence ensued. Fine, she'd disrupt their game of stalemate. Today she refused to play chicken!

"Hey Bro!"

"Hi Sis!"

"I came to see you before I get on the plane in a few hours."

He looked to be measuring his next words carefully. Still not moving from behind his big desk. He finally spoke. "Are you sure you want to do this?"

"Yes I'm sure!" she said curtly.

"You know you don't have to go."

"Yes I do!" She said raising her voice.

"No Bella! You don't have to prove anything to anyone," he said matching the elevated pitch of her voice.

"I have to prove something to myself. I am bigger and bolder than the best man in the industry."

"Ugh," he said as he pushed his hand through his hair. She knew he was controlling his frustration. She waited. "So what you haven't gotten your processes into a big vineyard? Success at the smaller ones can revolutionize what's possible."

"It's not going fast enough. You don't understand because you are a winemaker."

"You could come back to the winery and be a winemaker too or continue your research. Even though you left to pursue your doctorate degree, we can always use someone with your skills." He'd ignored her barb.

"No thanks Alejandro." She paused, lowering her voice. "You know I love you. My mind is made up. I only came to say goodbye before my flight leaves this afternoon."

He too lowered his voice, almost sounding resigned to fate. "I'm gonna really miss you."

"Remember we said we'd talk every Sunday!"

"Yes, and I mean it. Every Sunday! Starting in 2 days."

"I am just leaving. Surely we don't have to talk this Sunday?"

"That's exactly what I mean. Every week no matter what Bella!"

"Fine!" She wasn't a child. And she knew he would check on her.

"Okay, I'll give you a break this week. I do trust you Bella."

"I know you do. You're my brother, my best friend. I promise to do my job to the best of my ability."

"I have no doubt. One more word of warning. Stay away from those Spanish Casanovas. I don't want to have to come over there and kill someone for messing with my sister."

"Alejandro, you wouldn't!" She chuckled with amusement.

"Yes I would. When it comes to you, no one is good enough. Don't test me. Stick to being a nerd Bella. There's no need to cause an international incident or for me to drag you back to California so I can keep an eye on you."

"Yea, no worries," she said confidently. "This trip is all about my research. I don't have time nor a desire to play games or hook up."

"Very good. Now come give me a goodbye hug," he said as he rose from his desk and opened his arms.

She walked in to his big bear hug and suppressed the desire to cry. "Goodbye Big Bro. Love ya to the moon and back!"

"Goodbye Lil Sis. Love ya back and to the moon!"

She retreated from his embrace while quickly swatting away the tear that had escaped her from her eyelid. "I gotta go! No worries, Sunday's coming." She went to the door not turning back around.

"Yes Bella, in one week—next Sunday 5:00 pm, your time. I'll be calling. Make sure you answer."

That made her smile. She turned halfway around, searched his eyes, and swore she could see glistening tears in his determined look. "When have I ever not answered your call?"

"Never. Make sure you keep it that way."

She feigned ignorance that it was even possible to not obey him. "Of course my dear brother! Almost anything for you." With that pronouncement, she pulled the door open and escaped back into the hallway pulling it closed gently behind her. She slumped against that door, feeling drained with no energy to fight the tears now flowing from her eyes. I need to get out of here, she thought to herself. Looking around she saw the exit sign on her left. Ah yes, the back door.

She pulled herself away from Alejandro's office door and quickly moved into the stairwell. Somewhere in her descent between the fourth floor and the first level she got herself grounded. She'd found a tissue in her pocket and rubbed away the remnants of the tears. When she pushed the crash door open and walked into the sunshine, her determination to move on had given her new courage and strength. "Watch out world, here I come!"

Chapter 2

"Science means constantly walking a tightrope between blind faith and curiosity; between expertise and creativity; between bias and openness; between experience and epiphany; between ambition and passion; and between arrogance and conviction - in short, between an old today and a new tomorrow."
~ Heinrich Rohrer

Arabella descended the steps of the small commuter plane into the late afternoon sunshine. She was exhausted. Yesterday began her day of flying or maybe it really was today; she was no longer sure. She'd flown from San Francisco to London, London to Barcelona and then finally she'd arrived in Granada, Spain at the Federico García Lorca Granada-Jaén Airport. The clock on her cell phone said it was about 7:00 pm local time. All total, sixteen hours of travel, and after hours of moving from plane to plane, she could no longer think straight. She'd spend two nights and one day here at a local hotel getting herself acclimated. Monday morning, Gutiérrez Enterprises was sending a car to take her the last sixty miles to Jaén, her new home. Home maybe was not the right word—let me rephrase: Jaén would be her place of residence for the next six months. Yes that fit!

The CEO had planned to send a company plane to bring Arabella across the Atlantic. It was an idea he'd recommended only so she'd ride in luxury, and she refused the gesture. She considered it so wasteful when commercial planes were already scheduled to fly. Yet she'd didn't offer her opinion as to why she was declining the offer so as not to offend anyone right off. However,

Arabella was grateful her new employer suggested she not try to make the trek all in one day. First impressions were most important, and right now she looked like a sagging floor mop wrung out too many times. While business class might seem to be enough comfort for her journey, it was not. A hot shower and hours of sleep in a real bed would do the trick. Tomorrow she'd be ready to take on the world or at least by Monday she hoped the dark circles under her eyes would be gone!

Granada-Jaen airport was small and quiet. From what she could tell it catered mostly to tourists and locals versus big business. From the tarmac they'd moved the passengers down a stairway, and into a baggage claim area with enormous signage marking the places to see in the vicinity. Jaén's archaeological and nature preserves were on display, as well as Granada's historic sites. The region looked like a wonderful place to discover. Arabella sighed. Perhaps someday she'd stop working long enough to be a tourist who explored the world. Perhaps...and not right now.

The conveyor belt started making noise, a clear signal luggage was coming. When Arabella saw her two enormous roller bags, she reached over and collected them one by one. Thank goodness for wheels. With luggage firmly under control, off she went following the exit signs that took her outside into the evening sun in search of a shuttle bus stop or a taxi. She knew there were transportation options from the airport as they'd came in her work itinerary.

She'd also picked a hotel based on the company's recommendations list. All the places were centrally located in the city of Granada with no need for a rental car. Other than choosing one of the hotels off the list, she'd not done much else by way of research about Granada. Tomorrow, she'd ask about local sites for the one day so she could be a lazy tourist and get acclimated to the time change.

Just beyond the doors on the left curb she saw a taxi van. It was first in queue to pick up arrivals. She thought no need to take a shuttle bus when taxis were readily available. She walked to the vehicle's back door and the driver got out to meet her. He was an older man who looked to be a fatherly type.

"Buenas tardes Senorita."

Arabella switched to Spanish. "Buenas tardes Senor." After greeting the driver she gave her request to be taken to the Hotel Casa 1800 Granada. The driver seemed pleasantly surprised that she spoke in his native tongue. The value of education! Once her luggage was safely stowed, she followed the driver to the open door and climbed into the backseat of the vehicle.

As they pulled out onto the interstate, the driver continued to converse in Spanish. Maybe he was testing her to see if she knew more than the basic phrases or perhaps he was genuinely excited a foreigner spoke his Anadulsian dialect of Spanish. She'd done some business research about Jaén knowing the variant of Spanish was also prevalent in Latin America. She figured with the two cities being so close, they'd share the same dialect. A correct assertion it seemed. What she didn't know is if the similarity between Andalusian and Latin American

Spanish had anything to do with the Spanish colonization of the Americas over three hundred years ago. Perhaps she'd learn more tomorrow.

Interrupting her musings, the driver asked where she was from and what she did for a career. She saw no reason not to share those details. If he was going try to kidnap her, she'd rely on her martial arts training to fight back and protect herself. She silently hoped though that today would end uneventfully and that this man was a harmless person providing a service. He did seem impressed she was going to be working for the famed Gutiérrez olive oil company. He commented that he preferred their extra virgin olive oil best; and was expressed about other brands he also enjoyed.

She heard the driver pause. She looked up to see he was watching her from the rearview mirror. Oh no! What had he said? She smiled and said, "Por favor repitelo?" Please repeat?

He nodded and asked, "What are your tourism plans here in Granada?"

"I am passing through for business so I don't have time to be a tourist here. Perhaps one day soon."

"Such a tragedy Senorita. We have beautiful cathedrals and many sites of traditional architecture."

As they rode along, the driver gave some history—her hotel, built in the 16th Century, was in the Albaicín or Albayzín, the Moorish Quarter of Granada, and located near the City Centre. The area was historic and dated back many centuries. The entire Quarter was also now protected as a World Heritage site with many of its original buildings still intact and operable. He shared about the Flamenco dance shows she should check out, local wines to taste, restaurants to try and his strongest recommendation was not to miss seeing a place called "the Alahambra." She was working to process the names and commit them to memory. Truth be told though, right now being entertained, seeing sites and even what food to eat was not a priority. All she wanted was a hot shower and a bed for sleep. Okay maybe a couple of morsels of bread would suffice as she had no interest in waiting a few more hours to partake in a traditional Spanish dinner served after 10:00 pm at the earliest. She was grateful to the driver and it really did all sound fascinating for later. Maybe tomorrow. Maybe not. When the driver mentioned the Albaicín area is not accessible by car, she leaned forward. What? How would she get to the hotel? She interrupted him in a slight panic. What had he exactly said?

"Por favor, repitelo?"

He honored her request and explained the hotel itself is in Plaza Benal, up a cobblestoned pathway and it might appear hidden if one is just strolling by. No private cars and only very few taxis and buses were allowed to access Carrera Del Darro, the cobbled road on which the hotel is located. Once in the area he could get her close, but she'd have to go the final distance by foot as her hotel was situated on what they called 'a walking street.'

"I will park and help you the rest of the way with your bags."

She declined with a polite, "No thank you." That was exactly why she'd brought the wheeled luggage, unsure of what conditions she'd find and still she held a strong desire to remain independent.

Shortly after that bombshell, they arrived near the hotel. Arabella paid the driver, wished him a good life with abundant blessings, gathered her luggage and made her way to Hotel Casa 1800 Granada. True to the description, it was hard to tell it was a hotel, tucked away and nondescript. Just inside she went to the reception desk and checked in. She learned of the breakfast offerings and daily tea, including its free afternoon snacks. She asked about an on-site restaurant for dinner and was advised that they only provided breakfast and tea service. Immediately her face fell. Tonight she was exhausted and was going to forgo dinner. Then she had an idea. Were there any snacks and tea left from earlier?

The desk attendant said "hold on, I'll inquire." She lifted the phone and began speaking rapid Spanish with someone in the kitchen. Turns out there was some bread and fruit leftover. It was arranged to be sent to her suite. She took the offered keys and graciously thanked the woman. Out of nowhere a bellhop appeared and wheeled her luggage to the stairs. She followed close behind as he led her to her suite. Once everything was settled, including tipping him, she closed the door. She sighed a breath of relief. Finally at a resting point. Finally alone. Time to check out her digs.

Arabella looked around the room. The curtains had been drawn, robe and slippers set out, and a corner lamp left on. The bathroom held every amenity, toiletries and a nice big glass enclosed shower. She went to pull through her luggage for some night clothes. Just as she laid them out, there was a knock on the door.

She walked to the door and peered through the peephole. There was the same man who'd delivered her luggage, and he was holding a tray. She opened the door.

"Por favor Senorita, your tea service for the evening."

"Gracias Senor!" She went to give him another tip.

"No thank you. Have a good night." He bowed.

"Buenas noches Senor," she said as he let himself out, closing the door. Pronto service was amazing! She took the covers off the plates. Tea, fruit, bread, jelly, and they'd even scrounged up a few slices of meat to put into the bread. She snacked on the tea and made a small sandwich and left the fruit for another day. She re-covered the plates and set the tray aside. She then stripped out of her travel clothes and headed for a hot shower. In the bathroom she turned on the water, and found wonderful smelling soaps and shampoo in a basket on the counter. A dream come true!

After what seemed like a long rejuvenating steamy shower, Arabella dried off, wrapped herself in the complimentary terry cloth robe, and climbed into bed. She didn't care that her hair was still not brushed and wet nor did she bother to don her pajamas. Sleep...I just want to sleep! All tucked in bed, her final action was to send her brother a text message. 'I am here safe and sound. Super sleepy. Love you and talk in a week."

She got an immediate text back. "Glad you are there safe and sound. Call anytime you need me. Love ya much!"

"Sweet dreams!" She knew it was mid-afternoon in California. She turned off the ringer and set her phone on the nightstand, not planning to respond if Alejandro messaged back. If it was a true emergency he could call the hotel. She reached up and turned out the lamp, grateful for room darkening curtains as darkness enveloped the room even before the sun set. She was definitely going to sleep.

Chapter 3

"Science knows no country, because knowledge belongs to humanity, and is the torch which illuminates the world." ~ Louis Pasteur

The next morning when Arabella awakened, she jumped out of bed ready to begin a new day—renewed, alive and happy. I am in Spain, in my new world! She walked across the suite to pull open the thick curtains and peer out into the bright sunshine. It was 8:30 am. She saw the most beautiful old structure up the hillside. What is it? She wondered. It had such an allure, almost an opal iridescent glow. She was not much into history and didn't remember anything about sights in this region of the world. Plus, she was here to work, not play!

The world held so many places to explore and maybe someday she'd be restless with work and meander to places far and wide. In the meantime she could at least get a clearer look at this one. She closed her robe with the belt, unhooked the latch and walked out onto the balcony. The morning air refreshing without much humidity. Arabella knew it wouldn't last much longer as temperatures climbed with the sun. She curved her hand above her eyes to block the sun. She was curious about the complex; it had to hold some type of historical purpose and it didn't look to be ruins or in disrepair. She wished she could remember if the taxi driver had mentioned the place. Yesterday was such a blur. No need to rack her brain. She'd simply ask the concierge after breakfast. Her stomach must have heard her talk about breakfast…starving for real food! She turned and went back into her room, locked the door, and decidedly drew the curtains closed so she could dress. Once she was ready, she'd head out to breakfast and beyond to explore. Tourist for a day!

After a hearty breakfast, Arabella went to the lobby. There she found the concierge. "Buenas Dias Senor."

"Buenas Dias Senorita."

She continued to converse in Spanish asking questions about the structure she'd seen on the hill. She found out it is called the Alahambra and one needs tickets to get in. "Can you get me one ticket to visit sometime today?"

"Uno momento!" the polite gentleman said as he picked up the phone. She watched as he made three phone calls, frowning as he spoke in rapid fire Spanish.

When he came back to her he said, "Sadly no more tickets are available today." She was a little disappointed and he must have noticed. "You are not unlucky, Senorita. Tickets are usually gone months in advance."

"Thank you for trying! Perhaps another time then? I will be in the region for a while."

"Ah very good! Then there's no reason for you to swelter in the heat today—autumn and cooler temperatures are coming. Just remember to book the Alahambra ahead of time."

She made a mental note. "Since I can't go there, what else is there to do here for a day?"

She watched the concierge reach for a map that looked to be one of a large stack they have on hand to give to tourists. He said, "We are here at Casa 1800." And he drew an X on the map and circled it. Then said, "From here, it is a short walk to at least a dozen sites here in Granada, including the Cathedral, shopping district, the tapas area and many other historical buildings. You have traveled far so might I also recommend Hammam al Andalus, the Arabian baths. We are just a couple doors down and I am sure I can get you a reservation there."

"Oh?" She asked, "Are the baths like a spa?"

"Yes, precisely. They are wonderful. There you can have a soothing cold and/or hot bath and also a massage. I recommend you walk around town first and then go there later in the day or evening.

"I'd love that. Will you book me in for 6:00 pm?"

"Yes of course Senorita. I will arrange it and put a message on your telephone with details."

"Thanks so much. May I have the map?"

"Si! Of course." He said as he handed her the map. "Enjoy your day." He then picked up the phone to efficiently order her spa experience.

Arabella stuffed the map in her tote bag and headed out the lobby doors. A few hours of exercise and adventure was sounding more wonderful because spa was on the other end of the day. Maybe she'd have an afternoon nap/siesta. She was loving Granada already!

Chapter 4

"The olive tree is surely the richest gift of Heaven."
~ Thomas Jefferson

Promptly at five minutes to eight in the morning, Arabella arrived in the hotel lobby, dressed in a black suit, accented with a grey blouse. Her hair was pinned up in a bun atop her head, and she'd selected her black metal rimmed glasses to finish off her outfit—understated, yet professional. On this most important day, she would not be late. She was very good at following instructions and was intent to make a first impression that was fitting of her new role.

"Dr. Gomez?" A voice addressed her from behind.

"Yes," she said tentatively turning around.

"I did not mean to startle you. You are early! I am your driver, Ricardo. I will be taking you to Jaén to the Gutiérrez Enterprises estate."

"Hello Ricardo," she said as she offered her hand. "It's nice to meet you."

"I have the luggage you sent down earlier already stowed into the SUV."

"Thank you! It was not too much of a bother, I hope!"

"Not at all. I drove the larger vehicle. I selected it as we were unsure of how much luggage you might bring. Our journey will take about an hour with no traffic and it is my hope you will be comfortable."

"I am grateful for the ride, and in any kind of vehicle. I am sure it will be most comfortable."

"Si Senora. If you are ready, we can depart?"

"Oh, I need to check out and then I'll be good to go."

"No need. It has all been arranged by the company."

Arabella knew Gutiérrez Enterprises would pick up her overnight stays. She wasn't sure about expenses so she'd provided a credit card for incidentals. She supposed none of it was relevant. "Okay then, I am ready!"

"Please follow me just out front to the curbside."

She nodded her head in assent. Time to move ahead. The driver walked across the lobby. She turned slightly to look back over her shoulder once more at the hotel that symbolized Dorothy wasn't in Kansas anymore. She then followed to the waiting black luxury SUV where Ricardo held the door open for her to climb in. She glided inside to sit on the soft leather seats. Definitely not a hardship. This company must have clout if they were able to get legitimate access to drive into the City Center. Arabella had great memories of the little bit of Granada she'd seen yesterday. She did love the spa and last night's dinner was very good at a local Italian restaurant. She'd return here one day.

The ride to Jaén was scenic, filled with hill upon hill of olive trees, and homes peppered throughout the countryside. Ricardo, unlike the taxi driver, was silent. So she'd chosen to look out the windows while composing her thoughts and imagining a much simpler life than that of living in a big city. Next stop: Gutiérrez Enterprises - Jaén Headquarters Office! She was excited and nervous at the same time. In a few hours there'd be a formal board meeting. She'd be introduced, meet the management team and company officers. Later this afternoon she'd be taken to her temporary domicile—a cottage house on the edge of the estate. There as she'd been told, she'd find her company car. Arabella wasn't used to all these amenities coming with a position. None of it interested her. All that mattered was the opportunity to get to work on testing out her extraction approach, decreasing costs and enhancing the company's corporate position in environmentally friendly ways. A tall order, but one she was up for!

At exactly one hour after they'd left the front of the hotel, they pulled into a massive complex just off the highway. It was marked by a sign saying Gutiérrez Enterprises. It pointed the ways to the production facility, store, storage areas and the office building. They turned off in the direction of the office building.

"We've arrived Dr. Gomez. Welcome to Jaén," Ricardo said stopping the vehicle in front of a low rise building that was mostly concrete with glass strategically placed to blend into the natural surroundings. Very simple, yet chic! Arabella had simple tastes and was not a fan of flashy shows of money. She knew Gutiérrez Enterprises was a multi-million dollar business. Perhaps this first impression was telling her she'd selected the right place to come to work.

Before she'd realized, Ricardo had the door open and was offering her a hand down from the truck. She lifted her purse and shoulder briefcase and accepted his hand. "Thank you for the ride to bring me here. It was most comfortable."

"It was a pleasure. And I'm glad the ride was acceptable. Just inside the doors you will find reception. I will take your luggage to the cottage."

"Very well. Thanks again Ricardo," Arabella said shaking his hand. She then turned to face forward, telling herself no looking back! She took a deep breath and walked up the five steps to properly embrace her new future. Once she got inside to the reception desk, she spoke in Spanish. "Buenas Dias. My name is Arabella Gomez."

"Buenas Dias Dr. Gomez and welcome," the young woman said smiling up at her. "We've been expecting you. Mr. Fuentes will be down to greet you momentarily. Please wait here."

Literally two minutes later, a tall slender gentleman approached. He looked to be in his fifties, with distinguished gray highlights in his hair. In English he said, "Dr. Gomez, welcome to the company! We are grateful you are here. I'm Betram Fuentes." He held out his hand.

As she shook his hand, she warmly greeted her first coworker. "Thank you Mr. Fuentes. It is a pleasure to meet you. Please call me Arabella." Since he'd began their dialogue in her native language, she saw no reason to switch to Spanish for now.

"Very well, Arabella. I insist you call me Betram. We are very informal here in Jaén."

"Consider it done!"

"We will have a short board meeting to introduce you to most of the main players in our company. Then I'll give you a tour, we'll get your credentials, followed by a review of some reports. When it's all complete, you will be able return to your office or head out to the carriage house to get settled in."

True to Betram's word, her morning was a whirlwind. Earlier she'd met important figures in the family, including the CEO, one Juan Carlos Gutiérrez and many of the board members. She'd yet to have lunch or see the carriage house, and there were still a couple more meetings today. This was all fine. She was adjusting well.

Chapter 5

"To raise new questions, new possibilities, to regard old problems from a new angle, requires creative imagination and marks real advance in science."
~ Albert Einstein

Standing at the edge of the boardroom, Alberto Marcus Gutiérrez could feel the heat of desire flowing fast through his body. Who was she, the fiery red-head with a body of voluptuous curves sitting in his boardroom across from Betram, his cousin and Chief Quality Officer of Gutiérrez Enterprises? Even the dark rimmed glasses, serious look, and hair clipped up in a tight bun could not hide the passion she held tightly controlled in that black, smart business suit. A body like that should never be hidden in drab colors of black or grey. A body like that should be spread across his bed screaming out his name as he gave her endless pleasure. How long had it actually been since he enjoyed the frivolous company of a no strings attached affair? Perhaps it had been too long.

Reigning in his male libido, Alberto noticed they were pouring over what looked to be the latest laboratory reports he had ordered on the quality output of the olive oil production. Why did they have his reports? And why was he summoned in from the olive groves instead of continuing his watch over the delicate harvest operation that produced the delicate olive oil to which his family name is famous?

Alberto was renowned in the olive oil business. His traditional methods produced results over and over again and he was highly respected. At the ripe old age of thirty-five, the olive groves were all he knew in his native home of Jaén, Spain. Jaén is the source of almost three-fourths of the total Spanish olive oil production and he is proud to have an influence on that statistic. Most people in the world were not aware that olive oil production was such a lucrative industry and Spain is the world's leader overtaking Italy as the largest producer. With sun-bronzed skin tones, and a tall, muscular build, no one would doubt that he spent as much time in the olive groves as he did in the boardroom. He woke early and stayed up late to ensure everything went according to his plan.

"Oh, there you are Alberto," said Betram. "Let me introduce you to Dr. Arabella Gomez, a cutting edge scientist in the area of agricultural manufacturing."

Arabella looked up from the reports and noticed keen, golden eyes looking at her from the doorway. As if he knew he had her full attention, his gaze moved down her body in a slow perusal that felt as if he was undressing her right there in the boardroom. Then he again met her eye-to-eye as if to challenge her right to be here. A flash of amusement was quickly masked as he turned all business again.

How dare he? Arabella knew the type and did not appreciate the gesture. Rarely were men able to deal with her combination of brains and body. Through hard work and perseverance she had earned her way into the manufacturing field and still had something to prove. There was no time to be distracted by a man if she was going to make the kind of name for herself that would propel her to the top of her field.

In a few quick strides, Alberto was right there in front of her with his hand outstretched. He never took his eyes off hers as he walked. "Dr. Gomez, it is nice to meet you."

Arabella stared at his hand and thought twice about what might be accomplished from refusing to shake it. From what Betram told her, she and Alberto would be working closely over the next few months if she was going to accomplish her goals. Redefining the production process at this olive oil producer could revolutionize the industry. In her head, she said "just shake his hand, what could be the harm?" She put her right hand out and he clasped it in a firm, yet gentle grip. In that moment there was such electricity that passed from him to her. She felt his touch radiate up her arm. She stammered as she let go, "Please call me Arabella."

Alberto lifted his eyebrow as if he was unsure how to proceed. He said in a deep and amusing voice, "In that case Arabella, please call me Alberto." Arabella shook her head in agreement that they were now to be on first-name basis. The way he said her name set off warm sensations in the pit of her stomach.

Oh, she is very sexy and polished, Alberto thought to himself. A man could lose himself in her lush curves. Chastising himself, he asked why he kept thinking about her curves as if he had never kept the company of a woman before. Enough of this distraction. Alberto turned his attention to Betram. "Bertram, why am I here? As charming as it is to be in Dr. Gomez's company, I mean Arabella, I have important work to do in the groves."

Betram looked from Alberto to Arabella and cleared his throat. "The Board decided that we should redesign the production process. Not that there is anything wrong with the efforts you have undertaken and we are thriving. However, everyone agreed that now is the time to revolutionize what we do and how we do it."

Alberto sternly looked at Betram. "What are you talking about? I was not notified or called in to participate in the decision."

Betram again cleared his throat. "Alberto, I know this is difficult to hear. We recognized you would be an unknown factor in this scenario. One thing is for sure, we did know you would not be happy about the idea."

"If it is not broken, why tamper with perfection? And why is she here?" said Alberto as he looked over at Arabella.

"Yes, well the Board feels now is the time to innovate our processes. Dr. Gomez has been hired for her practical ideas and approaches to implement our new vision."

Alberto was fuming and barely able to control his temper. "I'll be damned, outsiders do not belong in my business."

"Yes, well the Board decided that she is our best shot at being able to move the plan forward. You may not like it and we expect you to work closely with Dr. Gomez."

"You cannot possibly expect me to work with her. I do not share my authority with anyone. I lead this operation and there is no room for anyone else, especially not an outsider."

Betram exhaled and spoke cautiously. "Alberto, the Board thought you might have an issue with their decision and that is why they sent me with Dr. Gomez. Let me outline how this is going to work. Dr. Gomez has been given full authority to implement whatever processes she deems necessary over the next six months."

"What? No way!" said Alberto.

"Yes, and she has been given full authority over your division of the company. So I recommend you play nice Alberto. Or else!"

"Or else what?" Alberto's voice stormed.

"Or else you will be permanently removed from your position and the olive groves. That will leave you with lots of free time to be angry. So you have a choice Alberto. Either you will partner with Dr. Gomez or you will be out!"

Arabella watched the dialogue back and forth. She hated the position the Board had put her in, and by the sound of it, it did not appear Alberto was any happier about the situation. In the end though, everyone would be pleased with the outcome if her approach actually worked. In the meantime, she just had to find a way to get along with Alberto. A way for him not to see her as an annoying woman. How hard could it be? He seemed passionate about his work. Who wasn't?

Alberto rubbed his hand over his face. He knew this was not the time or the place to argue. One thing was for sure, he would never report to a woman, with the exception of only one—his mother. And he was only willing to report in to her because she birthed him and deserved his respect. This ambush was uncalled for and he was sure it was this woman's fault! He didn't really consider himself sexist; he'd probably be just as angry with another who took his position.

"Bertram, this is not over. I will concede Round One." Then he turned to Arabella and smiled. "If you'll excuse me, I need to return to the fields." And he walked out.

"I'm sorry about that Dr. Gomez," Betram said with a monotone voice.

"Not a worry, and as I requested before, please do call me Arabella."

"Arabella, yes. Please let me know if you have any issues with Alberto. He can be a handful when his emotions take over."

"I am sure with time, it will get sorted out and Alberto will come around."

"I hope you are correct, and time will tell. In the meantime, again welcome to Jaén and the company. I've arranged for your executive assistant, Jose, to meet us upstairs. He will show you everything you need. We selected him as he came up through the ranks and is fully versed in the company as well as he speaks excellent English."

"Thank you Betram. I am sure he will be a wonderful help as I acclimate to everything."

Chapter 6

"A great fire burns within me, but no one stops to warm themselves at it, and passers-by only see a wisp of smoke." ~ Vincent Van Gogh

Late afternoon, Arabella was in the sunroom at the back of the cottage curled up in the window seat and staring out the huge panes of glass. In hand was a freshly brewed cup of Italian coffee. She inhaled the rich aroma. Ah Java, nothing like it! No work today, her first full day off. Lil Bella was half a world away from her life back in California. As she sat, she relived the moments since she'd arrived in the region seven short days ago...

Truth be told, it had been a long, hard week—her first days of work at the new company were full of tedious meetings and confrontations with the former Chief Scientist, Alberto. He was so frustrating, and he had no interest in making her feel welcome. She still had something to prove. And it had nothing to do with him. There was something exhilarating about being here, a sense of adventure in doing something new. She'd always limited herself in the past, unwilling to venture too far off the beaten path. To any outside observer it might seem she was a trailblazer. In fact, she'd pushed the limits inside the structures of home and family. This however, was different. Here she was on her own in a place no one knew her or her family name.

Most of the people here had been kind so far, offering her every amenity and convenience. The estate was beautiful and she supposed it was like its own small village with rolling hills and trees everywhere. She was genuinely thankful for the hospitality and acknowledged everyone in their native Spanish. That might be the winning formula—speak their language and they'll be nice.

She'd wanted to believe learning multiple languages, including Spanish and its variant Catalan might someday be useful. When she was young, her parents had insisted she be proficient in Spanish as many of the workers in California hailed from Latin American countries. So she began there, and added Latin while in high school to help in science and chemistry. She'd kept going and had mastered French and Italian during her undergraduate studies. Now she was well versed. Why not speak the romance languages—even if not practical, perhaps. It had definitely been an advantage here so far.

When Arabella called factory meetings, the workers listened as she'd spoken in their language and explained her approach. Alberto crept back into her thoughts. He had been present for each interaction and he still spoke to her in English sort of. That was okay and didn't distract her. Well maybe it did a little. She'd listened and especially appreciated his thick accent that made English sound like its own romantic dialect. She also didn't mind one bit he'd refused to see her as an equal. Likely he was trying to save face. This was his home, his company and his colleagues. She was an outsider. For now, she'd be compassionate for what he was dealing with. And even with all that, every time he was nearby, he'd gotten under her skin. On many of those occasions, he watched her with a grimace. She observed him from the corner of her eye scowling throughout most of her meetings. When it was over and crowds disbursed, he'd pop up right in front of her and say "I have questions." She'd respond "very well, please come to my office to discuss"' He always showed up, asked a gazillion challenging questions in his cynical and sometimes elevated tone, as he tried to convince her it wouldn't work. He waited as she'd answered all of them. She responded in detail with a rehearsed patience. It would work she always concluded. Nothing novel that a man was questioning her authority; he was yet another individual unconvinced her hypothesis was correct or viable. So be it! She had nothing to hide. Really, she had nothing to lose.

Alberto also intrigued her as a scientist. She'd read his resume and credentials. She'd even looked him up on the internet. He was extremely smart and understood the variations of agriculture and crop production. He'd been featured in European agricultural journals. The staff loved him, called him simply 'Alberto.' Why had he stayed in Jaén with his family? Why this role? Why wasn't he teaching at university? Did he feel it his duty to stay? His parents looked spry and capable. On a personal note, why was he not married with children running the hills? He had that rough and rustic look—the kind of charisma that put people on alert to pay attention when he walked into a room. If he wasn't angry, then he appeared to be in total control. As a man, he unnerved her in new ways with his handsomely brooding expression, too many a wrinkle lining his forehead and needing to be smoothed out with a smile. Did he ever smile? Laugh? Have a good time?

None of that is your concern! She said as she turned the coffee mug in her hand, enjoying the warmth and serenity of the moment. No reason to sour this idyllic moment thinking about him. You simply have to work together, coexist on the same property until you complete your mission. Focus on work! Yeah so what he is handsome and passionate about his work? Arabella refused to let him win. She'd prevail even if it killed her. She sighed. He will not win!

Turning to look out another window on the other side of the room, she appreciated the tranquil landscape. Her home away from home was quietly nestled amidst olive trees and hidden from the everyday traffic of people going up to the main complex. It had its own road too. Seclusion was what she needed—close to work with an illusion of escape. Inner peace settled over her. I love it here! I love days off!

The phone rang. She knew that ring. It was brother dear. Was it really that late on Sunday? As she reached for her mobile, she glanced up at the wall clock. Yep, he's right on time for our first weekly call. She pressed the green circle on the phone.

"Hey Bella, how's it going?"

"Hi Alejandro! All is well so far. And it's beautiful here."

"Of course it is going well. You're my sister and you're there giving it your best shot. There's no match for your determination, intelligence, wit and will-power."

When Alejandro talked like this, it reminded her of their parents. "Do your best," they'd said over and over.

Failure was always okay if you gave it your best shot. Small victories or big failures—none of it was meant to diminish one's efforts to do their best. She closed her eyes. She missed her parents so much. She missed her brother too. She could just imagine Alejandro sitting on the estate house's front porch with feet kicked up on the magazine rack. Mom had always hated him doing that—a habit he'd learned from dad. She couldn't believe she was homesick already.

"Sis, you still there?"

She swiped at a tear that had escaped during her nostalgic moment and cleared her throat. "Yep, I'm here."

"What's wrong? Are they treating you well? Being respectful?"

"Yes, of course. They are being very generous and kind. I just miss you. Really that's all. I was imagining you sitting on the porch with your feet up. It's Sunday morning and I know that's your favorite place to be.

He laughed. "Yeah Sis, you know me well! Feet up, relaxing a bit." He paused. "So I was calling to see if you're ready to come home? Do I need to come get you?"

"Well no actually. I like it here. I am not ready to come back to California. I was just thinking about how much I'm enjoying my efforts."

"Okay." She heard another pause in his voice. "Hey, you already know home is here for you. I mean, if things don't work out."

"Yea, I know. And things here are going to work out! You have my word on that." She was determined they'd work out come hell or high water!

"That's my Lil Sis!"

She smiled. If he'd been near her, he'd have picked her up and twirled her around like always when he was proud of her. "Just cause you're not here makes no difference. I got my twirl just now."

"Good! And on a serious note Bella, I have every confidence in you. I am just a phone call away. Hell, I'll jump on a plane at a moment's notice if you need me. You know that right?"

"I do my dear brother. I do not need to be saved. Let me repeat – I do not need to be saved! Okay, enough about me. How are you?"

"I'm making it. Business is good. We've started the crush for the Cabernet Sauvignon and Merlot grapes." She heard a little distance in her brother's voice before he stopped speaking.

"What's really going on Alejandro?"

He laughed out loud. "Bella, there is nothing really going on. Remember I'm the big brother who bosses you around. And you're the little sister who listens! There's no need to psychoanalyze me. I do miss you. Time for you to finish your day and me to go find some food."

She'd swear her instincts were right. But her brother was nothing if not stubborn. If he didn't want to tell her, he wouldn't.

"Sounds good! Goodbye Big Bro. Love ya to the moon and back!"

"Goodbye Lil Sis. Love ya back and to the moon!"

Just as quickly as their call started, it ended. And Arabella was content to stay right where she was, relaxing and enjoying the rest of the day off.

Chapter 7

"If civilization is to survive, we must cultivate the science of human relationships - the ability of all peoples, of all kinds, to live together, in the same world at peace." ~ Franklin D. Roosevelt

"I want to talk to you, my son."

Alberto looked up from his computer to see his mom standing in the doorway of the warehouse office. Those were some of his least favorite words, especially coming from a female. Frowning, he stood, and rubbed his hands down his jeans. His mom looked upset.

"What is it Mama? Are you well?"

"Si, querida. I'm fine. You never change. Worry first, even before you have something to worry about! It will prematurely grey your hair." She was scolding him.

"Yes Mama, I know. I'm glad you are good." He paused, and sighed. "Well then, come in and tell me what I have done to warrant you coming all the way out here into the groves."

She walked into the center of the rustic setting. "I did not say I was good. I said I'm fine. Anyway, I came to you instead of summoning you to come to me."

Moving around the desk, he stopped in the front of her, kissed her cheek, and gave her a hug. "Thank you, I think! It's not like you to come, and I am clueless as to why. What's wrong?"

"I will get right to the point. I want you to be kind to Dr. Gomez. I heard you have been hostile, downright nasty even. I need you to stop the assault."

"Mama, I cannot promise you that! She took my job!" It took everything he had not yell at his mother.

"Alberto, I get you are upset. And you still haven't adjusted to her new role. But don't be hot-headed. She was hired into our family business. First and foremost, we are family. It is for the best. You don't have to like it, and I raised all of you to have good manners. Use them!"

"But Mama, you are asking too much!"

"Really, my son?" With kind eyes, she reached up to cup his face with her right hand. He leaned his jaw into her gentle touch. "Listen to me carefully," she said. "I do know you. What makes you angry has nothing to do with Dr. Gomez. You're mad that anyone dare question your authority. She is a nice woman, very smart, and beautiful. Give her a chance to do her job."

"How can you say that? She is here, and now I spend most of my time trying to smooth over the impact of her decisions."

"Have you given her a chance? Have you even looked at how you can make her approach work? Or are you brooding over the Board's decision to implement her ideas for the good of the company?"

He sighed, ran his hand through his hair, and considered what she'd said. His mother was the only female to whom he listened. She had a point. He never stopped to consider why he was angry until now. People always gave him his way. "Perhaps you're right Mama. Okay, for you I will try."

"No try Alberto. Just do it. Your job is to make it work. And be nice!" She patted his cheek and smiled. "Show her what a charming gentleman you are!"

"Yes Mama, I will."

"Very good. I am sure you will thank me later."

"You're always right, Mama. I don't know how you will be right this time and I trust your wisdom. Now that I have given you your way, may I go back to work?"

"Yes of course." She raised up on her toes and kissed his cheek. Then she headed for the door. "Have a great afternoon. Oh and Alberto?"

"Yes Mama?"

"Come home for dinner tonight as I made almond cake for dessert. And remember what we discussed!!!" And then she was gone.

Alberto sat back down at his desk. Leaning back in his chair, he was in disbelief that he had agreed to be charming to Arabella. By no accident had his mother swept in and out like a breeze. She was so sure she would win the battle. He would bet his favorite dessert, almond cake, that Mama could sense his internal conflict over Arabella. Instead of letting him figure out how best to get rid of her, Mama had issued a command - be nice to her! If he was honest with himself then he would admit he wanted to do more than be nice to her. He wanted to tame her, brand her to himself and have her beg him to bring out her passion. Where did that thought come from? He rubbed his hands across his face. Enough! No work was getting done with all this being nice. He would grind this out later. Right now, Arabella could wait.

Chapter 8

"Sometimes I think the difference between what we want and what we're afraid of is about the width of an eyelash." ~ Jay McInerney

Bella was about to leave for the evening when Jose roamed into her office and put an envelope on her desk. "Senora Boss," as he liked to call her, "this was just delivered. I thought you might want to see it."

"Jose, what is it?" She asked looking at him while simultaneously holding up the envelope. She knew he was already aware of its contents. She'd given him permission to open all mail and correspondence unless it said 'eyes only.'

"Oh, that! Well it's an invitation to the company's ball next Friday night."

"I'm not going to any ball! I don't like those pretentious and fru-fru events where I have to dress in formal clothes and everyone stares at you for hours! This news could have waited. Anyway, first thing tomorrow will you please prepare a handwritten note with my regrets? I'll sign it and you can return the invitation to the appropriate party."

"I believe your presence is mandatory. But what do I know!" He shrugged as if he was already more informed than she could ever be.

She squinted her already tired eyes. "Why would my presence be mandatory? Spit it out Jose! What don't I know?"

"Perhaps you should look at the invitation." Jose had never been wrong so far from her estimation, so Bella put her glasses back on and opened the envelope. There in black and white was the invitation, written in English:

> *Please join Gutiérrez Enterprises in a celebration to welcome our new Chief Scientist, Dr. Arabella Gomez with a night of dinner and dancing....*

Arabella dropped the invitation on her desk and began to rub her temples with aching fingers. She was exhausted after a long day and was quickly developing a headache. "This can't be! There has to be some mistake. I don't need a party. I don't want to celebrate."

"Looks like everything is already in motion. And it's the end of next week. Better you than me!" He chuckled.

"We'll see about that! Have a seat." She was already reaching for her cell phone to call Juan Carlos on his direct line. Likely he was also working even though it was getting to be late evening. She took a deep breath. Be calm. As she sorted through the numbers, she could see Jose sitting smugly in her office chair being all ears.

Juan Carlos picked up on the second ring. "Buenos noches Juan Carlos, do you have a minute?"

"Si, of course. What can I do for you Dr. Gomez? Is everything okay?"

"Sort of. I just received the invitation to the ball for next Friday. There must be some mistake. It says I am the guest of honor. I wasn't consulted on this. I don't like parties. Tell me there is some misunderstanding?" She was again rambling.

"I apologize. Things moved quite quickly. Having the ball was my mother's idea. With her slow recovery from major surgery, I couldn't say no. She had already secured the doctor's agreement before she pitched the idea. The doctor is in favor of it and said she could attend for a few hours. Mama loves parties and is determined to honor your presence as our first female Chief Scientist. How can we disappoint her?"

"I see!" Arabella said without looking over at Jose.

"Would it really make you so unhappy to be formally welcomed and your work be recognized?" she heard Juan Carlos ask over the line.

"I suppose not. But I wasn't planning on attending any formal parties! I haven't been in Spain long and have nothing to wear!"

"Well my wife loves to shop for clothes, along with acquiring chocolate. I'm sure she'd love to take you shopping with her tomorrow. This is a work event and we've sprung it on you. The company will pay for everything. Would that be okay?"

"I suppose so! Yes, that'll be fine." She was trapped now like a caged animal.

"I promise we'll make it fun! Lots of dancing. No formal, stuffy speeches. Of course I do warn you, all our cousins will want to meet and dance with you. They are quite a competitive bunch!"

"Oh great! Well I'll make it work this one time. I understand the delicate situation with your mother's health. Next time though, please consult me first before believing I'm a yes."

"You have my word on it Dr. Gomez!"

"Please call me Arabella!"

"Yes, I apologize. Arabella it is. Lacey will be along to pick you up around 10:00 am. I'll have her give the details to Jose."

"Thank you Juan Carlos. Buenos Noches." And she clicked off the line and turned her attention to her smug assistant.

"Okay you win Jose. I'm going! Lacey Gutiérrez is going to call to set up the specifics of the shopping trip for tomorrow. Clear my schedule please."

"Excelente Senora Boss! It will be a wonderful time for you." He said steeping his hands together.

"Oh not so fast. You're coming to this ball too. If I have to work, I'm going to need you to tell me who's who!"

"I respectfully decline. You'll do fine without me."

"It's an order. We go as a team. Now, it's time for you to go home."

"Si Senora! I will go...to both the ball and home now. Have a good night!" He looked sullen with the news just like she felt.

It took all her composure not to burst out laughing at Jose's feigned pout. "Buenos noches Jose!"

She was no happier than Jose about this gala. Yet she knew it was a good idea to keep her boss and his mother happy. At least she wouldn't be alone with the sharks. She trusted Jose with her career. And that was better than being bait for Alberto to undermine her presence and her peace of mind all at the same time.

******

Sure enough the next morning at quarter to ten, Lacey pulled up in front of the building for the "Ball" shopping expedition. Arabella had gone into the office a few hours early even as she hoped Lacey had forgotten so she could put off the inevitable need to buy a dress. No such luck she discovered with Jose's announcement 'your ride's here!' The best she could hope for at this point is "nerd" girl meets dress shop owner, finds decent outfit and lives through said ball.' She got up from her desk, took her purse and told Jose she'd be back. As she walked out the main doors and down the steps, she saw Lacey wave through the sedan's window. And in the front passenger seat was another woman, so she opened the back door and climbed in.

"Hi Arabella! Meet Olivia. Olivia meet Arabella."

Olivia turned around in the seat and presented her hand. "It's nice to meet you. I'm also Javier's girlfriend and I hear this ball is to honor you and your much deserved new post as Chief Scientist. Congratulations!"

"It's nice to meet you Olivia and thank you!" She said smiling at the ball of energy known as Olivia, and shook her hand. Maybe this would be a tolerable experience after all. These women seemed welcoming and full of life.

Lacey interrupted her musings saying, "I thought we'd go together since we all need formalwear. It's no fun shopping alone!"

Arabella looked at Lacey through the rearview mirror, "I really appreciate your help ladies. I'm nerdy and studious, not a fashionista! And I'd rather not have to go at all, but I hear that's not an option!"

"Join the crowd," said Olivia. What? Arabella wasn't the only one who wasn't happy about going to the gala? That was good information to know even though it would do nothing to get her out of her current predicament as guest of honor.

"Now ladies, let's try to make the best of it. I promise it won't take all day. I've scheduled lunch and I brought along a box of chocolates to distract us along the way! Is that too much to ask?" Lacey sounded like her husband the night before!

"Definitely not," she proclaimed. All three of them laughed. Arabella let her guard down a little more.

Olivia chimed in. "Well we better get this over with."

Lacey put the car into drive and off they went. After going to numerous boutiques in Jaen, each of them found an ensemble to wear to the gala. Olivia had convinced Arabella to dress more feminine than business conservative. Today she'd done more shopping than she'd planned and wasn't overly comfortable with her purchases. They were very girly! But through it all, she now had developed real friends. They were almost like family, and had named themselves, *Tres Hermanas— three sisters!* Olivia, the romantic fairy tale writer; and Lacey the explorer—always with a box of chocolates to share! Her new sisters had donned her *Cinderella, Belle of the Ball*—this was her grand debut! While she thought they were crazy sending her into this fantasy, at least they promised to be there too. Just maybe she wouldn't have to pretend to enjoy the gala and could actually enjoy it. She hoped nothing like the real Cinderella story would transpire at this work event.

After lunch, Lacey dropped her back at the office with gold dress in hand and matching spikey heels. They'd agreed to meet up Friday midday for spa and makeup before returning to their respective locations to dress. That didn't seem too difficult to accomplish. At least for now, she was able to focus once again on work. Such a comfort….

Chapter 9

"When meeting, be the flame, not the moth."
~ Giacomo Casanova

The Night of the Ball …

"Oh my! How did I let my newfound friends talk me into such a mess? This so isn't you," she said aloud. Don't forget who you are, her brain added as she looked back at herself in the full length mirror. Contacts in, makeup done, hair pinned tightly in place, evening purse packed, shimmery spikey heels fastened, and finally—the dress! She stepped into her sparkled golden floor length gown with its cap sleeves, mermaid skirt, and side split. She hooked the top back and zipped the waist as she peered at her sideways image. "Ready Glamor Girl?"

She couldn't deny with other people dressing her, she stood out from the ordinary "Bella" of everyday anonymity. People actually might notice me tonight. Will Alberto notice me? Will he even be at the ball? His mother was probably demanding his attendance as a show of family unity, even though he might want to be a thousand miles away from her formal debut party as Chief Scientist. She knew from Lacey and Olivia some of the Gutiérrez family would attend. The subject of the ball hadn't come up during her work interactions with Alberto this past week, and she hadn't said anything. She didn't want to argue his opinion of her suitability for his position. Technically she didn't want to think about her enemy, Alberto Gutiérrez, where he'd be or whom he might bring as a date.

Then again, maybe she wanted him to be there alone, dressed to the nines and on neutral turf away from work. She didn't really consider Alberto to be her enemy anymore. For some even more bizarre reason she was actually attracted to him as a man. That was not something she was proud of and she'd tried to suppress her feelings for weeks. They worked in such close proximity. That must be why he was growing on her. Would he notice her as a woman tonight in spite of his anger for the position she held? Would he ask her to dance? What would it feel like to be held in his strong arms? Her face and other parts of her body were quickly heating up. Stop it Bella! You're a nerdy scientist who doesn't dance the night away! Take some deep breaths Bella. Regain your composure. This is a business event! Nothing more! Yeah okay...please tell my body that, she muttered aloud.

Backing away from the mirror, she chose to go sit at the vanity table, and reapply her lipstick. She glanced up at the clock on the armoire. Ten more minutes until time to go. The company was sending a car to pick her up. She wanted to drive herself and Jose was told "tell your boss, absolutely not!" No matter what she said, they'd pulled the 'this is for work' trump card. She'd finally acquiesced buying into the idea she should make an entrance since she's the guest of honor. The compromise was she only had to be chauffeured to start the evening. Once formalities were done, she could leave on her own. Juan Carlos wouldn't hear of her hiring her own car. Olivia and Javier had graciously agreed to drop her back home—technically she was living on the same estate as the palazzo. Plus Juan Carlos trusted Javier to be responsible for her safety—he's a rescue pilot. Arabella hated to impose on the couple's date night and she didn't need to be rescued. At the spa earlier today with Olivia and Lacey, Olivia dismissed her concerns as nonsense—they were going that way and it would be no effort at all to drop her at the carriage house. Again she conceded. Enough indecision! Arabella got up, picked up her small bag, and went to await her ride. "Time to put on a happy face!"

Chapter 10

"The emancipation of woman will only be possible when woman can take part in production on a large, social scale, and domestic work no longer claims anything but an insignificant amount of her time."
~ Friedrich Engels, The Origin of the Family, Private Property and the State

Arabella walked toward the ballroom, with her trusty assistant, Jose, following close behind. He'd met her just inside the hotel doors. She was still in shock from the throngs of photographers lining the entrance, all of them snapping pictures of those who dared step foot on the red carpet entryway. Click, click, click. She wasn't famous, nor interested in the press or the paparazzi. She'd have gladly come in a back entrance if she could have gotten away with it. Yet she graciously paused to pose and smile because she knew the publicity was good for Gutiérrez Enterprises.

"Senora Boss, I will make sure you know who's who in case you've forgotten." Jose said aloud.

"Thank you. I will do my best to remember all you've taught me about the names and where they reside in the family, government and industry." Jose, a God-send, had briefed her every day leading up to the ball so she'd be ready for formal introductions. She was unusually nervous as she prepared to step into the main event. What would tonight require of her? Being composed was one thing; being expected to perform societal niceties was something else. Juan Carlos, on behalf of the Board, had promised an easy going event. Already that notion was being tested.

Jose spoke quietly interrupting her worrying. "Might I add you look stunning tonight? I mean not that you don't always appear as elegant. It's just this evening...you are breathtaking!" Jose was fumbling over his words which was a rarity. It actually made Arabella stop mid-stride to look back at her trusted aide.

"Not you too, Jose? Remember behind the makeup and dress, it's just me, plain old Arabella." She was growing weary of the attention, people turning around and the whispers that she could hear as she walked by. It was bizarre to know they were talking about her. Who would ever want this kind of life?

"If I were older and didn't have a girlfriend, I'd quit my job and pursue you, Senora Boss."

"Somewhere in that there's a compliment, right Jose?" She chuckled softly.

"Oh very much so. Just be careful tonight as you are already the 'Belle of the Ball.' I know how Spanish men succumb to beauty. You will command so much more attention beyond the simple compulsory greetings."

"This is work! Nothing more. I'm sure I can handle any 'Don Juans' that come my way. Now can we please get on with it so I can go back to being an unassuming scientist?"

"Si, of course Senora Boss! You will do great!"

Arabella wasn't so sure. She had no time to analyze Jose's warnings. The grand ballroom doors opened up before her. How had they known she'd arrived? Show time! She stepped across the threshold and the music immediately came to a polite halt. Everyone stopped to stare as if expecting her arrival. Go figure, she supposed they were expecting her!

"Ladies and gentlemen, Gutiérrez Enterprises introduces our guest of honor, Dr. Arabella Mia Gomez, our new Chief Scientist." She knew that voice. It was Bertram, her first work colleague and someone who was fast becoming a friend. As she turned toward his voice on the right, she could see he was near the band on a small stage. He continued, "Let's toast to good times and good fortune for Dr. Gomez and the company. Salud!"

Arabella heard the many echoes of "cheers" and was stunned as she looked around the room. There must be hundreds of smiling faces with glasses held high--she was certainly on display! Like a robot she smiled and slightly bowed in acknowledgement of their toasts. She felt as if she was in a petri dish being inspected for her suitability.

"Dr. Gomez, would you be willing to say a few words?"

Jose had warned her they'd likely put her on the spot. She widened her smile and Jose stepped forward to escort her down the six steps and over onto the stage. Don't fall, don't fall, she mentally recited. As she came up onto the stage, Betram handed her a glass of champagne. She lifted her glass to salute Bertram, then turned to do the same with the crowd. Before proceeding she took a sip of the delicious liquid. Yummy!

This small speech she would make in Spanish to honor their culture and show everyone she was worthy to be heard. She stepped to the podium and microphone. "Thank you Senor Bertram and everyone. It is an honor to be here and to work at Gutiérrez Enterprises—such a distinguished company, with a rich history and dedicated workforce. I am excited to be given the opportunity to innovate an already amazing process. We will continue to work together to do good for the community and produce premiere products to sell here and around the globe. I appreciate everyone coming this evening to celebrate the company's success and my new position. Please enjoy yourselves, and I look forward to greeting each of you in person. Buenos Noches!"

She waited for the customary applause to end, then moved away from the podium and drank the remainder of the delectable champagne; then stepped off the stage and greeted Betram with a hug. "Thanks my friend!"

He replied, "You're most welcome Arabella! You belong here so I look forward to many more celebratory events! Now if you'll excuse me, I have a few more work duties before I enjoy the festivities. Duty calls."

"But of course. Have at it!" Arabella smiled knowingly as he walked away. Betram was ever the straight-forward one and also the first line fixer of all things in the inner workings of the company's corporate headquarters.

"You did very well Senora Boss!" Arabella turned and Jose was right there. He always found his way to be in earshot looking out for their business area. She was rarely ever alone to fend for herself. And for that he deserved every cent of money the company paid him. There were so many details to manage and just thinking about it made her head swim.

"I appreciate everything Jose! After another thirty minutes or so, greetings should be over. I can manage those on my own. So please take the rest of the night off. You've earned it!"

"Are you sure? I don't want to leave you with the piranhas."

"Yes. I'm sure. Notice has been served. I am officially Chief Scientist for the immediate future."

"Not that! I meant with all the men who now see you as both beautiful and intelligent! You will have to fight them off with a stick!"

Arabella giggled. "Now that's funny, Jose! I went from beautiful to smart in one breath. They'll be unhappy to know I'm turning back into a pumpkin at midnight!"

"You'll see, Senora Boss! Remember as Stephen Hawking said '[s]cience is not only a disciple of reason but, also, one of romance and passion.' Men have their passions and they could easily want to dance the night away with you. Many will want at least that and probably more!"

She wanted to change the subject. "Is your girlfriend here? I'd love to meet her. And then instead the two of you can dance the night away while I happily watch!"

"No, she doesn't like these pretentious events any more than you do!" He sounded pleased.

"You've picked wisely Jose," she surmised aloud.

"Si Senora Boss, I agree! A line is forming to greet you. I'll leave you to it. Call me if you need to be rescued or something!" It was his turn to chuckle as he walked in the opposite direction.

"I'll be fine! See you next week!" She spoke aloud to Jose's back. No sooner did Arabella turn around that she could see Jose was indeed correct. A receiving line as such had formed. First and foremost were her friends, Olivia and Lacey with their respective mates, Javier and Juan Carlos—two of the six infamous Gutiérrez brothers. Friendly faces! Yes! After that, there were numerous other faces that she didn't recognize, all of them seeming to stare at her—she supposed they wanted a turn to say their peace and check her credentials. She sighed, time to put on a gracious smile and get to it! As her mom used to say, "the sooner you do, the sooner you'll be done." Magically, a waiter appeared with a fresh tray of champagne—liquid courage! She picked up only one. It would be her last for the night because she was determined to keep her wits about her no matter the nerves currently plaguing her stomach.

******

"Dios, she's absolutely gorgeous," Alberto said as he watched the events unfold across the ballroom. His arch nemesis and new boss, Arabella, was greeting guests in celebration of her new position—which was technically his old position—still it should be his position! He hadn't planned to come, but he was told it was mandatory. Mama had also warned him to make peace. He wanted Mama to be happy or at least he didn't want her outwardly displeased with him especially since her recent surgery. Thus, he'd come under duress promising Juan Carlos that he'd brood and pretend to go along to get along. That had been his objective. Seeing her had totally altered his mood. While he was no saint and hadn't yet forgiven his brother or the Board, he wasn't as angry anymore—surprisingly not right this moment. Maybe it was the way she was smiling and acting so carefree. Perhaps it was the gown she wore—her skin laden in that shimmery golden fabric accented with a side split that showed off her leg all the way up to her bare thigh. If it were left to him, he'd peel the dress from her body to expose all that was wanting to be seen. Explored. Tasted... The lost art of seduction would never be wasted on Arabella. He was feeling his body respond to her slight gestures—the way she moved her neck, her gentle but firm handshake offered to those in the receiving line, the manner in which she nodded her head in agreement as the tight red curls that he knew loomed inside her updo hairstyle fought to escape. Even watching her drink golden champagne; he was sure his parents had ordered the finest money could buy, and all he wanted to do was lick away the taste from her lips and mouth so she only remembered the taste of him.

Perhaps Mama was right, things could look brighter if he gave it a chance. Truthfully, he wanted to know more about Arabella—body and soul. At the very least and no matter how tonight ended, he would indulge his libido with her very soon—she was the only woman to whom he had any current interest. No one here could hold a candle to Bella as her name bespoke. Since he'd already lost his job, not much else was at stake and he was in no position to take advantage of her. Since they'd been working in close proximity, he sensed that she too was attracted to him, and holding back. They were technically off the clock tonight and at a party where champagne flowed! No reason to hold back now!

Yes, finally the evening ahead is looking quite promising!

******

Time moved on and Arabella was still engaging with the never ending throngs of people. Did everyone really have to come say hello? She wasn't a popular kid in school. She'd left that honor to her brother and she'd certainly never perfected enjoying this ritual of making small talk. About fifty people into this and she was exhausted. Many shook her hand, others preferred to kiss both her cheeks, and those supposedly single men Jose warned her about also asked her to dance as part of their introductory greetings. She was as polite as possible and simply replied, 'perhaps later if time permits.' She had no interest in them. Still no sign of Alberto—the only man she had a passing fancy about. Maybe he's the lucky one to be anywhere but here.

"Dr. Gomez, it is a pleasure to meet you," the next person in line interrupted as he took her offered hand, held it up to his lips and kissed it. That was a bold move! Arabella almost snatched her hand away but then remembered she couldn't cause a scene. Maintain decorum! He continued to talk not at all bothered by her slight wince. "I am Antuan Frederico. I grew up just down the road from the Gutiérrez family. I am looking forward to getting to know you just as well as I know the family, if you know what I mean!"

"Senor Frederico, it is nice to meet you," she lied as she tried to wiggle her hand free from his. He was of no interest to her with his suggestive ideas and innuendo. Clearly he was still not trying to let her hand go.

"I would love to have your first dance this evening."

"No thank you. I'm not really into dancing."

"That's because you've not danced with the right man to lead you querida."

Unsure how to respond, she just smiled.

"Dr. Gomez, we are very proud of you! Hola Antuan!" She turned to see Mr. and Mrs. Gutiérrez next in line. Lifesavers if ever there were such people in life sensing she needed a rescue!

"Senor and Senora Gutiérrez. Thank you and please call me Arabella."

"Yes, very well. It would seem that Antuan is trying to monopolize all your time. Please do share Arabella with others?" Mrs. Gutiérrez said. Arabella immediately realized she would forever love this woman for saving her from this Antuan fella. She didn't need Jose after all.

"Senora and Senor! It is a pleasure to see you. You both look well. If you'll excuse me. Arabella, please don't forget what we discussed." Without another word, the gentleman disappeared.

"That was strange. Anyway, Senor and Senora, I appreciate all of this. I am a simple scientist and very honored to be here to work. But I didn't need a party to do a good job for your company."

"Nonsense Arabella," Mrs. Gutiérrez said. "You deserve every bit of this celebration and so much more. Women have often been left behind in not being acknowledged for their contributions to science, technology and medicine. We will not have that here in our family business."

"I wholeheartedly agree with my beautiful wife." Mr. Gutiérrez chimed in.

"I will continue to do my best. Enough about me. How's your health Senora?" Arabella wanted to know how she was progressing since having heart surgery last month.

"I am coming along. Very grateful to be out for a couple hours."

"Well you look good, so resting must agree with you."

"Yes, and my husband is quite attentive in reminding me of the doctor's instructions." Arabella watched her turn slightly towards her husband.

"Querida, but of course. It is my solemn duty to keep you with me—alive and well for all our days!" Arabella watched the love shine from one to the other. It was like they spoke their own foreign love language no one else could disrupt.

"You two are so cute and well suited."

Mrs. Gutiérrez reached for and patted Arabella's right hand with hers. "Yes, soon enough you will have a mate who dotes on you too. It is always better when two partner together."

Arabella cleared her throat not sure how the conversation turned in this direction. "Thanks for the advice. I'm not looking to settle down."

"Nothing you have to worry about for tonight. Who knows," Mrs. Gutiérrez said spreading her hand around the room, "your Prince Charming might already be here in our midst."

"I hope not. There are some unique, rather bizarre folks I've met just standing here."

"True indeed," said Mr. Gutiérrez and they all laughed as they knew it was appropriately directed at Antuan.

"Arabella, you have suffered enough. I am ending this line now!" Mrs. Gutiérrez held up her hand and from nowhere Betram appeared.

"Tia, how may I be of assistance?"

"Arabella has greeted enough people, please send regards down the line."

"Si Senora." Betram moved away as Arabella watched in silence.

"Arabella, please do forgive me for being high-handed."

"Nothing to forgive Senora, you are saving me yet again. Thank you!

"Go enjoy your party. And going forward, please call us Antonio and Catherine. Senor and Senora makes us feel old, and we certainly are not old," she said with indignation.

"Yes Ma'am! I mean Si, Catherine."

The older woman smiled, and Arabella kissed both cheeks for each of them. And off they went. When she looked around, indeed no line was left. The waiter did happen by yet again with more champagne. She refused and went off in search of some snacks; she was suddenly famished and wanted to prevent a headache from having drank alcohol on an empty stomach.

Chapter 11

"'My money's on the lady,' he drawled. 'You don't tame a vixen, you just travel in her wake.'" ~ *Lora Leigh*

"Here you are!"

She looked up from the bench from where she was sitting. Alberto was standing there in his tuxedo looking debonair and sophisticated. When had he arrived? She'd not seen him come in, not that she'd had much time to look around.

"What are you doing out here alone?" He'd said interrupting her thoughts. He actually sounded like he cared about her whereabouts and well-being.

"I needed some air," she said nonchalantly.

"Oh, were you not enjoying the reception?"

"Actually I was not. I don't really do parties."

"Why not? You are looking delicious in that dress. Every man in the room notices your fire-hot, red hair pinned tightly above your head, and this beautiful gold dress that fits you like a second skin. The music is melodic, and there are many men yet for you to dance. What's there not to enjoy?"

"What?" Her hand flew to her hair line as she pushed a lose curl back behind her ear. "I do not want to be noticed. I am not interested in them or their superficial desires. I only came to this party because the Board insisted it would be good for business. And this dress," she sighed and motioned to it, "…was Olivia's idea. She is such a hopeless romantic, that one. Writing all day long about love. She claims if I wore the dress to the party, it would inspire her to write. I had no clue how, and she said trust me. So here I am in this get up, wishing I were back in my lab, office, or almost anywhere else!"

Alberto, resisting the urge to reach down and pull her against his rock hard body to show her how much of a temptation she is, instead pushed his hands into the pockets of his slacks. He figured if he opted for a rational approach to communicate, then she wouldn't see that her innocence and controlled passion was undoing him moment-by-moment. She is, after all, supposed to be the enemy. Arabella took his position of power, and he had to accept her leadership. He wished his body remembered that fact, versus the insatiable desire to bed her. So what if she was the most beautiful and intelligent woman he ever met? A deadly combination if ever he saw one.

"I am sure Olivia has gotten her fill of inspiration. I saw her dancing the night away with my brother Javier after his surprise return from the latest search and rescue operation. Those two are quite a match. Never believed any woman could bring my brother to his knees. It's like she cast a spell over him. He used to stay gone all the time; now he moves heaven and earth to get back to her." He shrugged his shoulders. "Go figure!"

"Yes, Olivia is quite persuasive." She looked bewildered. "Hence, my current look and status."

"Like a devil in sheep's clothing!" He smiled. "If you are ready to go, perhaps you would like a ride back to the carriage house? I'm leaving to return to the estate."

Arabella could not be sure, but it sounded like Alberto was actually being nice to her. Should she trust him? Trusting good-hearted Olivia was one thing, trusting this man who had done nothing but undermine her authority for the last few weeks since her arrival, was a different story. Looking up into his suddenly impassive stare, Arabella said, "I don't know if that is such a good idea."

"Suit yourself! Olivia does not look like she is leaving anytime soon. Plus, I'm going your way. I promise to behave. I have not been gracious or accepting since I found out about you. And Mama has reminded me that she did not raise me to be rude. So, the offer stands."

Arabella thought to herself, how bad could it truly be? In spite of his rudeness, and lack of respect for her being his boss, he was a good man, respected in his community, with no criminal behavior on record. She knew, she had checked his personnel file. Everyone seemed to like him, even when he was being stubborn and hot-headed. It wasn't like he was going to dump her on the side of the road, or harm her. If he even tried, there would be hell to pay at home and with the company. She felt herself giving in. "Okay, Alberto, I will accept your offer of a ride."

Pleased with himself, he said, "Excelente, I will get the car and meet you out front."

"Thank you. I will go offer my goodbyes, and be along shortly."

By the time Arabella made it to the front, Alberto was waiting leaned up against the car. She was speechless.

Not just any car—a dreamy Porsche, navy blue, with a high metallic chrome. She was not impressed very often, and this car was beautiful. It had a sleekness, and yet controlled power that reminded her of its owner.

"Good, you finally arrive! I thought I might have to send a search party in to pry you away from the latest love interest." He met her at the car and opened her door.

She moved to get in the car. As if she had just heard what he said, she paused and tilted her head to meet his stare. "Hmph, very funny Alberto. I did not mean to take so long. I had to make a proper goodbye. I am new here, and what we are up to requires that I do not get off to a bad start."

He did not respond as she slid into the seat. He closed the door and came around to the other side. She was holding her breath awaiting his next retort. There was something about this man that pushed her buttons!

The motor purred to life and Arabella got comfortable in the passenger seat. Still he said nothing and did not pull away from the curb. In the silence, she noticed the soft tan interior and expensive seats. The low ride was not quite the same as the Mercedes-Benz sedan she had arrived to the party in, and noticeably the split of her dress agreed as it kept falling open.

She needed a distraction. "This is a beautiful sports car," she said.

He turned to face her in the car, and his eyes were drawn downward to appreciate the gap of her split that showed off her left leg, waiting to be caressed. I want to touch her, he thought. Noticing that he was staring at her body, he almost forgot to respond. Get a grip, Alberto, he said to himself and cleared his throat. "Thank you. I like this car. And, you are correct. In Spain, it is very close knit and business deals are put second to relationships. I grew up here so I often forget what outsiders must deal with to fit in. I offered to give you a ride, and it does not bode well for me to have a tantrum when you have responsibilities I am fully aware of because of your position. I make amends. How about for one night we call a truce?"

Arabella considered what he said. "I would like that." She reached over and offered her hand for him to shake. Instead of shaking her hand, he lifted it to his lips and kissed it gently. Then he let go, turned back to face front, started the car, and off they went. She was again rendered speechless. She turned her head to stare out the window. Get it together girl, she whispered to herself.

The ride to her new home was quiet, except for the sound of the Porsche's engine as Alberto expertly moved them along on the curvy roads. He was like a precision racecar driver speeding on the open highways in one of man's finest creations. Just off the main road was the family estate surrounded by olive groves that stretched for miles. One more turn and they pulled into her driveway, where he brought the car to a stop.

"Let me walk you to the door," he purred.

"I'm fine, it is only a few steps from the car. Thank you for getting me home safe and sound."

"Ahhh, in spite of your impressions of me, I am a gentleman. I will walk you to the door."

"Fine," she said refusing to argue. She was tired from all the preparations to get ready for the evening's activities, and sick of the dress that kept falling open. She was confused by how nice he was being towards her. The sooner she got into the house, the sooner she could stop thinking what it would be like to kiss Alberto. She was not hired to have an affair, and certainly not with him.

Being a gentleman as he said, he came around the car, opened her door, and offered his hand. Gathering the two pieces of the dress together in her left hand, she gave him her right one so he could help her from the low ride car. When she was safely on her feet, she began walking toward the door. He placed a hand at the small of her back and led her forward. She was getting hotter with each step

"Mademoiselle, here you are as promised. Might I have the key to open the door for you?"

"Absolutely not! You have been gracious enough for one evening. I surely am able to open my own door."

"I insist. When asked about tonight, you will have to say I delivered you safely and was the perfect gentleman."

"Fine," she said again. She looked down into her small, gold colored evening bag and pulled out the key. She hesitated a moment before she handed it over to him. Their fingers touched slightly and she felt a sizzle of electricity. She gazed up from his hands into his eyes.

She saw the red hot passion that resided there. Damn, he is irresistible!

As if in slow motion, she watched his head lower so that his lips touched hers. One simple gesture, except that she chose that exact moment to lick her lips. Not only did he capture her lips, he tasted her tongue. He stepped toward her and she stepped into his embrace. He had big, strong arms, the kind that one gets from lifting weights or doing manual labor. The kiss went deeper and deeper until she lost all consciousness of time and she was out of breath. Just when she knew she would die, he pulled away from her and took a step back. She felt flush and weak on her feet.

"I think we both got a little carried away. Let me get the door." Arabella just stared at him as he made quick work of opening it. Had he really kissed her right here on her doorstep? Arabella felt like some teenage school girl home from a date. Except this was no date. This was Alberto, her enemy. It sure didn't seem like he was her enemy when they were kissing. She was defrosting inside and not sure what was going on. She needed time to think, to suppress whatever had her allow that kiss.

He moved out of the way to let her pass into the house. She paused and then moved her molasses feet. Just as she turned to shut the door, he stepped forward making it almost impossible to close the door.

"I did not mean to kiss you. I could not resist."

"Alberto, I do not know what to say."

Standing just inside the entry way of the carriage house, he pushed the door closed. "Querida, you do not have to say anything. I find myself taken aback by you. I saw an opportunity to kiss you, and I took it. Let me be straight, as you Americans say. If not for the fact we were in front of this house, on my parents' estate, I would have made love with you on the porch. I will not let a door stand in the way of getting what I want. As ironic as it might seem given our positions and brief history, I want you!"

"Why?"

"Why what?"

"Why are you interviewing for the position of my lover Alberto? You of all people are the last person I would expect to want that job. Remember all that talk about how everything is my fault? That I took what was yours? That we are enemies?"

"I am a proud man, Arabella. And I am not without flaws. There is something about you that stirs my blood. I mean other than my resentment for your taking my rightful position. When I come into the room and you are there, I am immediately aware of your presence. I want you next to me, near me, actually I imagine you on top of me. I am not comfortable with it, and yet it is so."

"Really?" She said smiling. Not quite sure what was to become of this conversation and enjoying the banter. "You think I am a woman who wants to be on top?"

"I would bet all I own that you want total control in and out of the bedroom."

"You might be right about that Alberto. Nothing is worth doing if you aren't gonna strive to be the best."

Unsure of her mood, and out of his element with her, Alberto decided to keep it playful. "I will let you be on top in my bed."

"And in the boardroom and the groves?"

"Ah, that my sweet one, is debatable. I never relinquish total control."

"I bet you don't. Me either. So, we are at an impasse."

"How about we compromise? Tonight, I make love to you, and neither of us is on top. Tomorrow will work itself out."

"Look Alberto, it's late. I appreciate the ride home, and let's just leave it at that." As if just hearing what he said, she replied, "Wait, what compromise? Who said I am going to sleep with you?"

He laughed. "You are fun! Now, with all seriousness, please let me clarify. I do not want to sleep with you. I want to make love to you. And I promise if you say yes, on this night there will be no sleep for either of us. Plus, the stars are in alignment. You want me just as much as I want you. I don't believe you have any interest in hiding it. Business is business, and sex is sex."

"You might be right. So what?" she went on to say nonchalantly. "I do not always act on my wants."

He reached out and lifted her hand turning it palm side up. He kissed her wrist with the most sensual move any man had ever laid on her. She heard herself say, "Mmmm."

"Si querida, this is what you want?" He lifted his eyes to gaze into hers. "There is plenty more from where this comes. Let me show you." He turned her one hundred and eighty degrees to face the mirror she had forgotten she was in front of. He pulled her body back into his, and she leaned her head back against his shoulder. He whispered into her ear. "I would start here at your neck and kiss you." He kissed her. He moved his hands to pull her hips into his erection. "Do you feel how much you excite me?" She shook her head up and down. Then he kissed her right earlobe, and she closed her eyes. He moved his hands to her breasts and said "Arabella, open your eyes! I want you to watch." She did as he asked and stared back at him. Her pupils dilated and she wanted more. Just at that moment, his hands found their way to caress her breasts and drawing circles. She watched him pinch her nipples and felt them harden to the point of aching. He was driving her insane. He whispered again into her ear, "I want to taste you, all of you. Please let me make love to you."

"Yes, make love to me."

His eyes flew to hers. "Say it again?"

"Alberto, make love to me. Right here, right now."

Not needing any more encouragement, he spun her around to face him again. He lowered the zip of her dress and let it fall to the floor. There she was, an exquisite creature wanton with lust. This first time would be quick because he could not contain himself. He would make it up to her next time. All he knew is he had to be inside her now. He unclasped her bra, as her breasts spilled out into his hands. He let it fall to the floor just as he did the dress. All that remained was a thin gold lace thong that would not stand in his way. He lowered his head and captured her lips beneath a brutal and possessive kiss. She would know him as a fierce lover, insatiable for her and she would beg for more! Arabella was squirming in his arms. She threw her arms around him and was kissing his chest. Oh god, I must slow this down, he thought. Before he could, she unzipped his pants, and pushed his pants and briefs down. As if he could take anymore, his erection sprung free, and she reached out to stroke him.

"Querida, if you do too much more of that, it will be over before I get inside you." She ignored him. He grabbed her by the hips and set her onto the table. Their lips found one another again and in one swift motion he pushed into her. This was heaven. She was tight and moist. In and out at a frantic pace he held her close. He could feel her about to come. Hell, he could not hold on anymore. One last push and they went over the edge together.

******

The next morning, Arabella awoke in the bed wrapped around Alberto, her once enemy. Awkward! How do you get yourself into these messes?

"Good morning, querida." It's as if he sensed she was awake.

"Good morning Alberto," she said as she got out of the bed, put on her robe, and went into the bathroom to throw cold water on her face. What now? Go back out there and make him leave. Last night shouldn't have happened. It was amazing sex though. One night only, remember that is what you promised yourself? Arabella brushed her hair, took a deep breath and went back out to her bedroom to face the music.

"So what's the verdict?" he said as soon as she opened the door.

He'd stopped her dead in her tracks. "What are you talking about?"

"Do you want me to go?" He said in such an honest voice.

"Go?"

"I know you're conflicted."

"Yes, I am conflicted! I want you to go. No wait, stay! I don't know what I want you to do. I need to think!"

"Well querida, I'll do whatever you command me to do."

"Yeah right! We'll see how well this new leaf goes when we get to the office on Monday. Somehow I doubt I'm that lucky!"

"If memory serves you got lucky a bunch of times last night."

"You are incorrigible Alberto. Will you stop trying to annoy me? What happened last night was really great sex. And we cannot do it again."

"I enjoyed myself too. And please tell me why not? It was hot, passionate, amazing! You are alive in my arms. Totally different than the facade of cool, collected and composed you demonstrate in the boardroom."

"I don't want to talk about this anymore. I came here to implement my ideas, and make lots of money for your family. I did not come here to sleep my way to success!"

"If it makes you feel any better, we did not get much sleep last night!"

"You take my words and manipulate them to get what you want."

"I'm hurt querida! Your intention is to slay me with your words. Are you complaining about last night?"

"Look Alberto, I think if you want to stay, then we need to change the subject. Let's just enjoy this time together."

"Okay Arabella, for now. I won't ruin our weekend."

"Thank you," she said as she climbed back into bed.

Chapter 12

"One cannot think well, love well, sleep well, if one has not dined well" ~ Virginia Woolf

After an amazing round of sex, and a quick nap, Alberto was awakened by the light being switched on. Across the room in the doorway there she stood looking like an angel bearing gifts. When had Arabella left his side?

"I brought us some food," she walked into the room wearing a summer dress that accentuated every curve from her chest, to her thin waist, and to the hips he'd caressed as she rode him to orgasm. Feeling his erection stir to life. He thought, damn she is beautiful, and she's mine. I want that.

She smiled at him, as if hearing his thoughts. "You hungry? I'm starving."

Not wanting to go there yet, he looked at the tray. "Where did all that come from? When did you leave?"

"Chef texted me about thirty minutes ago to let me know your mom had made her world famous lasagna and insisted on sending me some. Your mom thinks I work too much and need to eat healthier. So I met him on the doorstep downstairs. She always sends way too much."

"Well, she's probably right about you working too much. You spend many hours in the lab."

"I know, only men can be excused for working too much, right?"

Attempting to lighten the suddenly serious mood, he said, "I didn't say that. It just leaves little time for you to cook me meals."

"That's funny," she said. Even though she did not like the idea of women being relegated to slaving over the hot flames to prepare meals for men who don't know how to come home and do their fair share, this was not a conversation for this moment. "Well anyway, here's food for us to share." She put it in the middle of the bed and looked down. "Oh, I forgot the bread. Be right back."

When she returned, she could see Alberto had made a plate and set it on his lap. "I've returned."

"Welcome back," he smiled. "So I can get you to bring me dinner as long as someone else prepares it?"

"Yes, I am a scientist, not a chef."

"I grow olives and I like cooking. I'm good at it."

"Okay that's good news so don't expect me to cook for you."

He smirked, "Mama always says that the way to a man's heart is through his stomach."

She rolled her eyes and threw a dinner roll across the bed at him. "You are ungrateful. I am not interested in getting to your heart Alberto. As a matter of fact, I don't even know why I bothered to bring this tray. You can have your stupid stereotypes about women."

"Whoa I am only joking with you. You are so sexy when you are angry. Come here to me and I will serve you."

"I am not a love sick puppy you can spoil."

"Oh, the things I want to do to you. I promise there is no doubt that I would ever mistake you for docile, subservient puppy or at my beck and call. Please Arabella...come eat with me. There is no point in wasting the food Mama has sent over."

"Only because I don't want to disappoint your mother, will I join you." She laid across the bed, and he scooped food on a plate for her.

"Thank goodness for my mother. She makes the best lasagna even though we are Spanish. When my oldest brother was very young, there was an Italian family who came to live with us. They were caretakers. The father, Luca, a landscaper, and the mother, Francesca, was a fantastic cook. They had two children, Rosa and Luciano. Francesca and Luca became best friends with my parents as they grew the vineyards in the early years. It's how I got my name, the modern version of course. Luca's second name is Alberto. It means 'noble and bright.' Mama says in the hours after I was born, I had this bold, bright look in my eyes. She said I seemed as if I would have great purpose, amass wealth for those around me and be a leader. So she wanted my name to symbolize that idea. You see, Mama has a vision for all of us. When she mentioned her thoughts to Francesca, her friend said she could see my bright light too. Francesca mentioned about how she had looked up Luca's names when they were dating and that's how she knew the meaning. Somewhere in their conversation she suggested my name be Alberto. Luca means bringer of light. So, his two names, bringer of light, bright and noble was a good sign. It was even funnier when my middle name was chosen as Marcus. However, Mama and Papa never had much to say about the origin of Marcus" He paused. "I think both her and my mother had too much free time."

"I think they were very wise. You are a great leader who has brought immense wealth to your family's vineyards. With my input, it can only grow."

"Perhaps," he said as he forked lasagna in his mouth.

"What, you do not think my approach will be successful?"

"I think I am in bed, eating mama's lasagna with beautiful you and I don't want to talk about business." He leaned over and briefly kissed her lips before she could get another word out. "Now eat so I will not feel guilty having you for dessert!"

Feeling her body heating up at the touch of his lips on hers, she knew it was pointless to talk business. "Okay bright one, you win this round. No more business tonight, and tomorrow is a new day." She wondered to herself what had happened to Luca, Francesca and their children. She would ask later, much later after dessert…

******

Sunday was a blur. Alberto left sometime late Saturday night and Arabella had been able to compose herself once more. Thankfully, her brother sounded distracted on their check-in call. That was very good news! She didn't want to talk about the ball nor her activities after. Best to not give Alejandro any fuel for the "come home" rant. When she got off the phone, she deliberated over what she'd do tomorrow when she saw Alberto in the office. He wasn't out of her system yet, but he wasn't worth losing her job over. Back to business as usual would be the sage advice she'd follow.

******

"Arabella, can we talk?" She heard Alberto's voice from her office doorway. It was only half past eleven. She was sure at least one day would go by before she had to deal with him and the impact of her wanton behavior. Clearly she'd miscalculated.

"Now is not a good time," she said as she continued to stare at her laptop.

"Please?"

She still didn't look up from the laptop even though she'd bet her paycheck he was not going to go away. "How did you get past Jose?"

"I told him that I had some reports I needed him to pick up for me from the laboratory. He was happy to go."

That made her look up. "You had no right Alberto. Jose works for me!"

"You're right. I'm sorry. I just needed to see you so we can talk."

"I don't want to talk. I told you it was a one off. Now please get out of my office so I can finish my work."

"No, we need to discuss what's happening between us."

"Look Alberto, there is nothing happening between us. I had a weak moment, and acted on it. We were attracted to each other. We had sex a few times." Well Arabella thought to herself, it'd been more than a few times. It was a few times that first night. "I'm better now and got you out of my system."

"No you didn't. Don't lie to me Bella."

"I am not lying. You're an attractive man, and you can have anyone you want. Except me. Now please go away!"

"We can discuss this here or at your place tonight. Which one do you prefer?"

She glowered back at him. "Fine, come over tonight! And for the record, I was happier when we were enemies. I had some control."

"I wasn't happier and if you think about it, you don't really mean that!"

"Bye Alberto. Out! I have work to do."

"See you tonight querida." With that he was gone. Arabella was frustrated. Not because he'd shown up, but because he was right. She still wanted him and was almost desperate to have him! She needed to figure out her next move before he arrived at the carriage house later this evening. And she would come up with a strategy or so she hoped.

Chapter 13

"I don't want comfortable. I want passion. I want someone who will kiss me like it's the only thing keeping him alive." ~ Author Unknown

Two Weeks Later...

"Hi there!"

Arabella looked up from the stack of papers she had been engrossed in to see Alberto taking up the entire doorway. How any man could be that handsome, she did not know, but he was—sexy from head to toe, with a smile that would devastate even the sun. It was like a déjà vu moment similar to when he'd appeared weeks ago in the same spot and demanding they talk. Needless to say, that talk ended with them back in bed not just that night, but many more nights thereafter. Talk is cheap anyway, right?

"Hi," she said tentatively and just a little too breathlessly. Arabella was rarely unsure of herself, and here she was unable to utter a greeting in his presence. She cleared her throat, hopeful the dense fog would lift from her brain too. Why this man rendered her speechless when she was alone with him, she'd yet to sort out. Probably some hormone she didn't recognize or know how to suppress! "Why are you here Alberto?"

"I figured you would still be here working past the time when normal people go home!"

"If you are alleging I am not normal, I will remind you, you are also lumping yourself into that category!" Her eyes sparkled with a smile even though she held her lips tightly pursed together.

"Touché, Arabella!"

She loved the way the "r" in her name rolled off his tongue. Much lower, her body stirred to life. Oh hell, who was she fooling? She loved everything his tongue did!

"So if I am not normal, what am I? Abnormal? Strange?"

"Oh no, you are different. There is something about you, not just your workaholic ways or determination to do your best. I don't know how to describe you...you are just..." He paused. "You are SPECIAL, unique, precious."

"Wow. Thank you!" She was blown away by his description of her. "Now, why are you here?"

"I brought you dinner."

"You cooked me dinner?"

"Nope. I didn't say that. Cook made it."

"Veggies too."

"Yes, I told him to pack enough for two as I didn't have time to eat with the family tonight. I didn't mention I was going to share it with anyone."

"That doesn't bother me. It was very thoughtful of you to think of me."

"Bella I think of you all the time. I probably don't have the most decent thoughts every time. For the most part though, my thoughts of you are work-related and wholesome."

She blushed and then got up to walk over to the window putting her back to him. "Alberto, clearly you get I am a serious businesswoman and scientist. Why don't others think of me as such?"

"What makes you ask that question?"

"I don't know. It's just the meetings I had today were quite tedious. It was like they'd rather have talked only to the men in the room, and not me. Having the meetings was my idea, and with the agenda I created."

"You must know that you are a queen. You can have any man you want! They admire you—your brains, how successful you are, and of course your drop dead gorgeous looks all wrapped up in your fiery red hair. They think of you as a complete package, and unlike me they don't get to spend as much time together working with you."

Arabella turned to Alberto and flashed him that look that said I will have my way with you! But she would not be undone. "Yeah so what they admire me as a woman. Men have followed me around like puppy dogs since I was ten and started to develop breasts."

In that moment Alberto's eyes wandered down to her full bosom, and all he could imagine was rubbing his tongue across her nipples.

Arabella cleared her throat. "Excuse me! Eyes back up here please. You have a one track mind when it comes to women."

"Si, querida. I am a hot blooded Spanish man. We are a passionate bunch! And I could make love to you right here on your desk."

Pacing the floor, she continued ignoring his suggestion. "As I was saying Alberto, why don't they take me seriously? I have every bit of grit and tenacity that they do. Just because I am a woman does not mean anything. I can outlast them and I will win!"

She was so sexy when riled up. "Arabella, look at me?" She ceased her pattern of back and forth and faced Alberto where he sat in the chair. "Please stop your tirade! Why do you care whether they're taking you seriously or not? You did not care whether I related to you seriously and you took my job. It does not matter. You will present your case for action and they will cave in and give you your way."

"Sometimes I wander Alberto, how you got my attention. You are so matter of fact. Now that you have it, now what do we do?"

Alberto could think a few things he wanted to do with her—to her. However, remembering why he came by, he said, "Let's eat dinner?"

Chapter 14

"But I believe above all that I wanted to build the palace of my memory, because my memory is my only homeland." ~ Anselm Kiefer

They worked through dinner, sharing information about the day. Arabella wanted to steer the conversation away from business. "Tell me more about your family?"

He shrugged. "My family? Well, we're like any other family, ordinary and boring."

"I doubt that is true. Just indulge me. With the exception of the work meetings and the ball, I haven't had much interaction with them."

"Okay, let's see. You are already aware of the family business and how it works for the most part, and who is responsible for the formal roles. And you know I have five brothers and no sisters. Also, I'm sure you've heard about my mother being sick a couple months ago. Everyone is now worrying about Mama just like she has fussed over us these many years. All my brothers came home for her surgery. We were a consolidated front to support her and Papa. The doctors are pleased with her progress and expect her to be good as new once she fully recovers. Mama gets tired very quickly, and still she acts like she's never been sick a day in her life."

"I'm sure you all are watching her every move."

"Yes we are. My brother Javier has stayed on to give me additional help looking after them."

"Your parents are lovely people. They've been welcoming though I've only been in their presence a couple of times. Even while your mom has been sick, I never feel unwelcome on the estate and she sends food daily."

"Yes, that's Mama—a good caretaker no matter what. On plenty of occasions we've had to shoo her out of the kitchen to go rest!"

"That went over well?"

He laughed. "Not really! Her determination outweighs logic at times. Papa has taken the brunt of her wrath. She doesn't really listen to the rest of us. She says she's the mother and we are the children. We try our best not to boss her around!"

"I'm sure you and your brothers are quite charming and know how to sway her."

"On rare occasions perhaps. Mama and Papa watch over everyone in one way or another. They always make sure new people are welcome and included. I saw you being introduced and dancing with a bunch of my cousins at the ball."

"Yes, I got to meet so many people at that ball. Now, I need an organizational chart to remember all the names and relationships."

He laughed a hearty laugh. "Sometimes I need one as well."

"Your brothers have all been welcoming and kind when I run into them too! And I must say y'all are fascinating to observe."

"How do you mean?" He said even though she saw the spark of amusement in his eyes.

She continued. "I noticed you all have endless fun at each other's expense, playing and talking like you have a secret language."

"Si! We do. We are a big family as you might have discovered. Though we are geographically dispersed to many parts of the world, we are very close. The antics are non-stop amongst us brothers—always teasing each other, joking around and pulling pranks. I find it quite amusing too. And we spend a lot of time in trouble; not as much as when we were children. When others are around, we are low key—intent on not dragging them in. That is with the exception of our cousins who grew up around us—they too have become like brothers and they are fair prey."

"Yes, I've witnessed some of it."

"I hope you were not caught up in anything serious."

"No, not at all. For now, they seem to spare me at the office. I guess I am too new yet. At the ball, some of them seemed to be in competition to dance with me. I didn't mind it so much. However, I did feel like the shiny new toy at times."

"I will talk to them and ensure that never happens again!"

"No, please don't!" She said placing her hand on his arm. "I can take care of myself."

"Yes, I'm fully aware of that. I do notice how well you take control. Like in the Director's meetings when our male egos take us off track, you reign us back in. Or when we are in the fields and someone has changed the protocol, you are direct, yet confident in re-demonstrating your approach."

"Thanks, I think!" Even though she knew she would not apologize for her role, she was sensitive to the fact that she was an outsider in a close knit family and company.

"It is indeed a compliment querida. I may not have wanted to acquiesce my fields and laboratory to your leadership. Yet, I see what you are creating might be a huge opportunity for us to revolutionize our industry, bring more prosperity to our communities, and expand our business in sustainable ways."

"Wow, I thought we were talking about your family!"

"Business is woven into our family."

"Yes, I suppose you're right."

He must have sensed her mood shift. He reached over and put his hand on her cheek. "You started this inquiry, what else do you want to know?"

Even with his kindness, Arabella had previously identified the questions she needed answers to from him. Since he asked, she saw no reason not to ask. Plus, she'd done the most risky thing anyway when she'd slept with him. He'd proceeded to caress her cheek. It was damn hard to concentrate. "Okay. Are there girls in this family?"

"Yes, and not nearly as many as the number of male offspring."

"Did your parents grow up here in Jaén?"

"Si, they were born and raised here."

She hedged her bets and asked one of the most important questions that she'd wondered about. "Why did you stay here?"

"You mean why did I not move to a big city like my brothers?"

She shook her head yes in response.

"That's a good question. I thought about staying in California after my formal education ended. For the first couple of years of college, I was homesick. Then before I knew it, it was time to graduate. My parents asked what I was going to do. Then I remembered why I went in the first place: I trained so I could come back home and help my family, our neighbors and region. I guess it just made sense to be here. So here I am," He said as he spread his hands out.

Ask him, her inner voice chimed in! As if on autopilot, she heard herself say, "Why aren't you married Alberto?"

"You have an interest in filling the position?"

"That's not why I'm asking."

"Oh? Then why?"

"Clearly you are not a playboy. I see how women look at you. You're intelligent, handsome, rugged, and strong. You have a sense of loyalty to family and duty. There should be legions of women on your doorstep. Yet, there are no lines. Why not?"

"Probably because I still live in my mother's house. Not many women find that attractive. Mama is a force to be reckoned with."

"So you're a Mama's boy?"

"Hell no. That's Marcelo. I just spend much of my time focused on our work. I have in the past had girlfriends. They just lose interest in my work, then I lose interest in them. I am easy to get along with too. My passion or as some might say my angry temperament is either a take it or leave it endeavor."

"I can see this. Your tough exterior might intimidate someone without the confidence to stand up to your arrogance."

Alberto laughed. "Yes, I will admit I can be arrogant at times!"

"And righteous!"

"Hey, I thought we were talking about my family. When did this become a "pick on me" event?"

"No one picks on you? You say what you want with passion, and then you disappear for others to pick up the pieces!"

"Perhaps now you can see why I'm not married. "

"I guess. It all looks like a facade to me! You are not really like that when it's just the two of us. Or when you are with your brothers. Well at least not most of the time from what I can see. Yes, you brood, and think too much. Yet you are kind and loving."

"Thanks querida. What about your family?"

Arabella could feel the hairs stand up on the back of her neck. Don't say too much. She got up from the couch and went to stand at the office window, her back to him.

"What is it?" She sensed he had come to stand behind her. "Tell me?" He said as he gently put his arms around her. She leaned her head back against his chest.

"Not such a happy ending. My parents are dead. They died within months of each other. My only sibling, a brother, lives back in the States. You can hear we are a much smaller family than yours."

His grip on her tightened. "I'm sorry to know your parents have passed away."

"It's okay. Death is part of life." She wished she really was okay with it all. Best not to say anything else. She forced a smile onto her face and turned in his arms. "I'm here now and there is a lot of life around me!"

"Yes, you are a part of our family now. Everyone who comes onto this land becomes family. And plus, I like having you around!"

"No you don't."

"Si querida, I do. Maybe not in the beginning. But now, I definitely can't get enough of you!"

"Oh you just like having someone to fuss with."

"Yes and do this with." He lowered his lips to hers and clearly their talking was over. She was grateful for the distraction. It wasn't long before they'd made it out of the office and back into her bed.

Chapter 15

"A friend is someone who knows all about you and still loves you." ~ Elbert Hubbard.

Arabella's cell phone rang. She'd just shutoff her laptop, and was planning to head home. She saw it was Olivia.

"Hi Arabella! Got a minute to talk?"

"Hi Olivia! Yes, I was just finishing work for tonight."

"I know this is last minute, and you might have plans. But will you attend my wedding ceremony? It's a small gathering of family this Friday at Noon. And sorry for the short notice. Javier was adamant with Mama G that we have our wedding as soon as possible. He doesn't want us to be apart anymore." She knew Olivia called Javier's parents Mama G and Papa G since they'd insisted not being called Senora and Senor or anything formal.

"Congratulations Olivia! I am happy for you two and honored to be invited. But I have to work."

"Please Arabella. I don't have any living family members and really only have you and Lacey as my new friends here in Spain. It would be nice to have someone on my side of the chapel."

She liked Olivia and Lacey. The days leading up to the ball were fun. "Well I suppose I could take a long lunch. Yes, I will attend."

"Thank you so much for saying yes!"

"It really is my pleasure. You know sometimes I forget there is life outside of work."

"Yes, we all have those moments!"

"Enough about me. Do you need any help with anything? Do you want me to come early?"

"Nope, I am keeping everything low key and simple. I found a dress that fits. We're not having a reception. The ball was enough of a party for us. Plus Mama G is still recovering from surgery. After the ceremony we'll have an informal lunch. Then we'll stay on for another day or so before heading back to paradise for our honeymoon start on our island."

"That sounds wonderful."

"Yes, my husband-to-be says he's been patient long enough and it's time to marry me."

"Yes, I can only imagine." Arabella's thoughts drifted off to Alberto—he was definitely not ever labeled the "patient brother."

"I can't, but I think Javier worries I might change my mind. I won't, but he says now is still our time."

"That's super romantic. I will be there with a heart full of happy wishes for you two!"

"Thanks again for agreeing to be there. Have a good night. Sweet dreams my friend!"

"You too Olivia!" And she pressed the end call button.

Wow, Olivia and Javier to marry! Seems like another brother would fall to marriage. That would make three—Marcelo, Juan Carlos, and now Javier. Statistically fifty percent within a year. Those were high odds.

Chapter 16

"Life is a song. Love is the music."
~ *Wisdom Quotes Community*

Weeks later…

Arabella was standing at the door fidgeting. She kept nervously looking at herself in the mirror. Alberto hadn't provided many details when he'd called to ask her to go out for a night on the town. They'd arranged for him to pick her up at seven-thirty. She'd debated back and forth. Was this a 'date?' He didn't call it a date and they'd never gone on a real one before. She didn't count dinner after work and the times they'd ended up in bed as a 'date.' On those occasions, she'd always worn what she already had on.

Tonight she'd donned a simple black dress, stockings and crimson wrap, hoping the attire would be considered 'appropriate' for their 'date.' She'd left her hair down with tamed curls set off her face and pushed over her shoulders; she'd put her contacts in so she didn't have to rely on glasses, and applied a modest amount of makeup. Her dress fell an inch above her knees, and had an understated elegance. Mama always insisted Arabella pack a little black dress 'just in case.' That was pretty much all she had here in Spain anyway, except for a few business suits and some casual wear. Oh there was one exception she'd almost forgotten…that scandalous gold dress she'd worn to the ball. The same dress that she'd had on when Alberto seduced her in this very entryway. Memories of that night came flooding back. Arabella felt her body stir to life and overtake the nerves. He was so masterful at reducing her brain to mush. All he had to do was touch her and she turned into a woman she did not recognize—so desired and seeking their mutual pleasure with reckless abandon. She caught a glimpse of herself in the mirror.

"Look at you," she said aloud. All wanton now! Why are you so unhinged? It's Alberto, an agricultural scientist like you. So what he is liquid fire on a pile of tinder? He wants to go out with you to a public place. Tonight you will see what he's like in a more social setting with no business talk to distract you. Oh gosh! Is this a good idea? Scientist or not, he could be dating with fashion models and actresses who are way more polished and provocative. Arabella peered back into the mirror. Her inner voice said, it's time for you to really look at who you are! He chose you, for whatever reason. Blinking back she saw herself standing there—you're smart, determined and feisty! She liked that description of herself. Not nerdy and meek like she'd been all these years. Tonight, she'd be a new Bella...even if only for a few hours. She'd be the woman in the gold dress from the night of the ball. Confident! Yes, confident in her desirability; irresistible and ready to discover what a 'date' with Alberto would be like. Good! She put a smile on her face. Now, it's time to relax Bella and find something else to do while you wait. Smoothing down her dress one last time, she turned away from the mirror in search of a distraction.

At exactly seven-thirty, Alberto pulled up in a black Ferrari as Arabella sat on the front porch perusing a magazine. Well not really. She'd been waiting and practicing deep breathing exercises more so than paying attention to the magazine and its contents. That was 'the something to do' she'd used to occupy herself. She set the magazine aside and didn't move. Watching Alberto emerge from the car was a treat. He was as handsome and delicious as ever; hair freshly washed and combed back, clean shaven and dressed in all black. There was even a red handkerchief adorning the jacket's breast pocket. It was like the devil himself had arrived to claim her—sinful and divine all rolled up into one person....

She smiled and tentatively rose from her sitting position on weak knees. "Hi you!" She said as she again smoothed down her dress. "Nice car!"

"Good evening Bella. You look amazing," he said as he approached to kiss her on both cheeks. He ignored her comment about the car. She ignored it too as she inhaled his scent. He smelled of sandalwood and lemon. Oh what deliciousness she thought as the aroma played havoc on all her senses. Alberto placed his hands gently on her hips and stilled her slight swaying motion. I guess he did notice her brief desire to faint. Was it possible to be intoxicated without drinking or doing drugs? With Alberto, yes!

She looked up into the amber embers of his eyes. They burned into hers and she quietly whispered "good evening to you too. And thank you for the compliment." Those words were pulled from her brain as she fought for rational thought. Why was she so lost in the depth of his eyes? Why was her body heating up so fast that it was taking the chill out of the early evening air? Why is it so hard to breathe?

All questions went out the window as he leaned in to kiss her lips. She'd instinctively closed her eyes, weaving her hands around his neck. He tasted of black licorice, like the liquor anise. If he'd not been holding onto her she'd have fallen down. Seconds of kissing turned into minutes. His hands had found their way lower and she'd pressed her body closer. They were inseparable. If they kept this up, they were not going anywhere in public. Not that she minded being the center of a man's attention. It was a novel idea for her, and she liked it. Or at least she liked being the focus of Alberto's desires.

A sense of logic must have prevailed for Alberto as he ceased kissing her and leaned his head to her forehead. Inhaling and then he said, "Bella Mia, we'd better stop before this ends up with us in bed."

She stepped out of his embrace. "Yes, you're right. I just need to get my handbag and lock up."

"Wait, before you go, I have something for you." She paused and saw him pull a jewelry box from his jacket. He handed it in her direction.

"No thank you," she said without taking it. She turned again towards the door and he caught her elbow.

"What? I don't understand. Most women don't turn down gifts of jewelry."

She turned fully around ready to face off. So much for their date night and being the center of his attention! He'd said the wrong thing. "I am not most women Alberto."

He met her gaze and she saw the wariness lurking there. "That's true! And Bella trust me when I say, I don't want you to be anyone else. I only want you."

"That's lovely. And I can't accept a gift from you!"

"Why not?"

"You work for me. It would not be appropriate."

"Says who?"

"I said so. It wouldn't look right." She bit her lower lip, now present that her nerves were on edge again.

"Bella, you better come up with a better argument than that. You cannot use the boss-employee excuse as a defense. We are sleeping together. So your reasons do not hold weight."

She stopped to ponder his words. He of course was right again, she admitted to herself as he stared back at her. What now? She stalled by pushing the hair that had fallen forward back over her shoulders. She quickly inhaled and then let the breath out. Might as well fess up and come clean with him. "Okay fine. I have a rule to not let a man use gifts as a way to buy me. I am not for sale. Nor will I ever let anyone use me. That includes you Alberto. I've worked too hard to get to where I am and I'm not going to be swayed by nice talk, sex or gifts."

She watched him run his hand through his hair. And then he spoke. "Arabella, I respect that and you. Look at me and hear me! I admire you, your desire to make a difference and willingness to compete against the best of the best. Trust that I have no interest in using you, nor do I think you could ever be bought off."

She wanted to believe him. And she wanted to understand too. "So why the gift?" she asked as she pointed to the box that stood between them."

"This?" He held up the box. "I got it especially for you. It reminds me of your fiery spirit. Open it and see for yourself?" He pushed the box forward again.

Arabella tentatively took the box, and opened it. Inside lay an orange and red glass medallion on a silver chain. With its oval shape, it shined like flames of a fire, iridescent and inviting as it caught the light. She instantly loved it. She'd realized all the intensity of the moment had left her breathless.

"Do you like it?" he asked softly.

She looked up into his shimmering eyes, knowing he was looking into her soul. He'd seen a lot about her in such a short time. "Actually I love it. It's beautiful."

"It's Murano glass from Italia. I saw it yesterday afternoon as I walked by a store in town. I had to have it for you. Even if you had not accepted it, I would have kept it to stare upon and think of you."

"Thank you. I apologize for my behavior."

She watched as he pushed a curl back that had escaped over her shoulder. He then smiled. "Ah querida, there is nothing to apologize for. It is your fiery spirit that is the exact inspiration that had me buy this gift." He then leaned forward and placed a gentle kiss on her lips. "Now, we best be going."

"Wait, I want to wear it tonight! Will you put it on me?"

"Of course. Anything for you Bella!"

She held out the box for him to remove the piece, turned around and lifted her hair. As he slid the necklace into place, her heart melted. No one had ever before been willing to see into her spirit and challenge her at the same time. No one until this man.

Once the necklace was secured in place, Alberto lifted her hair from her hands and gently smoothed it back down. She held her new medallion admiring its smooth curves. He then turned her around and she looked into his eyes. She saw that shimmer again. Damn he's gorgeous.

"Ready?" he said.

"Yes, I'm ready," she said. He pulled her back into his arms are kissed her so passionately.

******

They'd ceased kissing and finally made it to the car, on their journey away from the estate. Alberto promised her he'd have his way with her after their night on the town. Just this once, she'd acquiesced to his logic. She really did want to go out with him on their date night. And she was curious even though she had no details to where he was whisking her off to go. Maybe now was a good time to ask. "Where are we going Alberto?"

"I am taking you to dinner and then to Flamenco, where we will watch the most seductive, romantic dance you'll ever see."

"I've never been to a Flamenco," she said as she watched him maneuver the car over the countryside roads.

"You are in for a real treat. No two Flamenco dances are ever the same, even if performed by the same people."

"How does one know what to do if every dance is different?"

"The dancer spontaneously moves with passion and expression. It is art performed before one's eyes—a love song of reverence and submission to the beat that goes beyond music and touches one's soul."

"That sounds beautiful."

"Yes, just as you are Bella!" He glanced his head away from the road to her and then returned his attention back to the black pavement. "Perhaps we will practice our own dance later tonight!"

Arabella could feel the heat rise. She couldn't get used to his compliments. Most likely because they came with a promise of passion and actions to come. Alberto did nothing halfway. Best not to think of that promise of seduction. Stay on topic she reminded her brain! Right! "Well I'm sure I cannot dance the Flamenco."

"I could teach you!"

"I have two left feet."

"No you don't. You danced perfectly in the arms of many at the ball."

"It just seemed like I did."

He laughed out loud. "You are mistaken querida. I watched every move you made as you danced with those other men. Even with my cousins who are not the best dance partners. You are a natural!"

Arabella paused for a second. Had he just said he'd been watching her? "What do you mean, you watched me?"

"I could not keep my eyes off you. The way you looked in that gold dress blew me away. Your red hair like fire! I wanted you, and there was no way I was going to let any other man have you. Not that night."

"I am not a possession Alberto!"

He reached over to touch her cheek with his index finger, gently caressing her skin with his soft touch. "Trust I am fully aware you are alive and real, not an object. The way you fall apart in my arms, leaves me with no doubt."

Her heartbeat kicked into overdrive. How was he driving through all of this? He moved his hand to shift the car gears. They were driving fast, and she chose to remain quiet. The scene was like something out of a modern day fairytale, and she knew she was continuing to fall under his spell.

Perhaps he took her silence as his cue to continue. "I am no good at sharing, as you already know. That night, I was afraid someone else might be unwilling to let you go once they had discovered you. You are a jewel."

"I am just ordinary me."

He was silent. She wasn't sure he heard her pronouncement. He pulled the car to a stop on the side of the road. He shifted the gear stick to park and turned to look her in the eye. "Bella, there is nothing ordinary about you! You are a brilliant woman. Even if I hate to admit it, your expertise and skill in our science is pure genius. Your beauty rivals no one else, even as you hide beneath glasses and often times frumpy clothes. You are articulate and compassionate, even when the people you encounter are being condescending and asinine, like I was."

"Wow no one ever said such nice words to me."

"They probably wanted to and you wouldn't let them into your world."

"I let you in!"

"Yes, you did." He reached over and took her hand lifting it to his lips. She instinctively closed her eyes and sighed. When she opened them, his were piercing into hers.

"Querida, you are a gift to my life and I'm unwilling to turn away from this, from you."

"Thank you. I don't know how to explain what's occurring between us. And I like how we are together."

He leaned over and kissed her. A gentle kiss that still left her wanting more and breathless when he ended it.

He grumbled. "We better get back on the road if we are going to make our dinner reservations."

"Yes, each mile seems increasingly difficult!"

"There will be time for us later." He restarted the car and moved them back on course. They rode the rest of the way not saying a word.

Dinner was at a quaint little tapas restaurant in the middle of Granada's old town. It was on a square full of life, shops and lively entertainment. All during the meal they'd chatted about life in Espana. They both seemed happy enough to not bring up anything significant, including work or science. Alberto was just a normal guy and she'd let her guard down for a night on the town.

If Arabella wasn't careful, she was going to end up fat from all the eating she'd done since coming to Andalusia. Tonight's feast was decadent. First wine, freshly baked bread and olive oil. Then the first of many small plates. Her favorite dish was the peas, with diced ham. Courses moved forward to salad and a main dish of salmon served with potatoes and sautéed spinach. Her little black dress was in protest by the time dessert was served. But who could turn down chocolate lava cake? Her new friend Lacey, Juan Carlos' wife, says 'one should never resist a little chocolate decadence.' Since Arabella was in the presence of a man she considers decadent, and he'd made the recommendation she thought why not indulge in the lava cake too! It was amazing, even more so when

Alberto rubbed the smudge of chocolate from her lips with his napkin. She could just submit to pure temptation right now. Not a good look in public for someone with her position. Sometimes she wished there were no multi-million dollar company, no title, or science between them. What would it be like to be man meets woman, have them get along, and all be well in the world?

She felt a gentle touch on her hand as it sat on the table. "You ready to go?"

"Hmmm?" She said as she heard his voice.

"You're a thousand miles away. Are you ready to go to our next stop querida?"

She wasn't sure. Yet she wasn't trying to share her latest thoughts. "Yes, I'm ready."

"Let's go." They departed the restaurant and returned to the car.

From the car park in the center of town, Alberto drove them up the mountain to the caves where they'd see a Flamenco show. He explained along the way that many of the dance venues were once homes. They'd been converted into small clubs where the dancers performed two or three shows each night. Some served dinner or small plates but people mainly came for the dance.

Arabella was game for a lot in life, and she felt like tonight she was a tourist in someone else's dream. Alberto seemed not to notice she lacked confidence in many social settings. She certainly was not the life of the party. Given a choice she'd prefer to stay home and watch television. Yet and still, she was grateful he'd taken her out to show her some of his customs and culture.

Before long he pulled the car into a space, and got out to escort her. She looped her arm through his and they strolled inside. The hostess showed them to a table for two in the front and near the low stage. The place was dark and cramped, reminiscent of a cave for sure. There were tables for couples and small groups. This place held an ambience meant for intimacy.

Shortly after they were seated, and ordered drinks, the lights dimmed even further. The only glimmer emanating from the burning flame of red bottle candleholders on each table. The wax had dripped down the glass making its own artistic statement. Music from a guitar started. A spotlight turned on, and clapping began. One lone dancer appeared in the center of the light—a female dressed in a form fitting red and black dress. She held a fan spread out across her face. Her dark black hair pinned up in intricate layers, and accented with a decorative hair comb. When the music picked up, she began to move to the beat. Never still, she sauntered along weaving between the tables, carefree and dancing. When she was five feet away from them, she began to stomp her feet and dance at the same time. How does one do that? The movements look impossible.

At some point, a man dressed like a matador joined the woman. Arabella watched those dancers, mesmerized by the almost out of control passion that the music evoked. Was she the bull, the cape or the temptress? All Arabella knew was it was breathtaking and indescribable. When the show ended, she turned to Alberto. "Thank you for an amazing night."

"The pleasure was mine, querida."

Going on a date was wonderful! Leaning in, she whispered in his ear. "Please take me home now and make love to me."

"Yes ma'am! I promise to make passionate love to you all night."

He did just that as a man true to his word—many times that night in her cottage. Arabella was weak with all of the attention he showered on her body. He was versatile and creative—exposing her to different experiences. She never backed down and they experienced immense pleasure together.

That night Bella slept so peacefully in his arms, desired and sated by the one man who she couldn't get enough of—Alberto.

******

The next day, Arabella was in her office reminiscing over their date. It was nice they could spend the night together, even though she didn't expect him to stay. I wonder what it would be like for him to come home to me every night. Or better yet, for him to be at home waiting for me to get in from work? That would be a huge victory for feminism if a man like Alberto stayed home and she was the breadwinner. Not going to happen, she surmised. And it sounded juicy good. She did not think she would make it past the hallway before he had stripped her of all her clothes. He had already stripped her of every vestige of sanity she had when she arrived in Jaén.

Dismayed by her lack of focus, she said aloud, I should be doing my work, not living some fantasy. Just over from the lounge chair where she rested was her desk, and all the reports of analysis from the olive samples that awaited her review. She sighed heavily and dragged her tired body to her office chair. She plopped down on the brown leather and picked up the report at the top of the stack. She looked down, and paid no attention to the writing on the page. Hmmm, I wonder what it would be like to wake up next to Alberto each morning. Would they always make love before going to start their day's activities? They had every morning so far. Or would the thrill and passion wear off and they bore of each other? Arabella why are you talking out loud, she chastised herself. This is ridiculous! You are being ridiculous! It's an affair. Nothing more. Soon there would be no relationship, so stop thinking long term? Get back to work!

Her cell phone rang. She picked it up. It was Alberto. "Hi Querida, what are you doing?"

She smiled. "You already know what I'm doing. I'm working. What are you doing?"

"The same!"

"Yes, figures. May I help you with something?"

"Si! Say yes to our spending this evening together."

She sighed, already knowing she was going to say yes. "Yes!"

"What do you want to do?"

"If it's okay with you, I'd like a quiet evening in tonight."

"Me too. I'll pick up dinner and see you at nine?"

"Yes. See you then."

"I miss you querida."

"Alberto stop trying to distract me. Get your work done and see you tonight!"

She heard him laughing as he clicked off their call. Focus Bella, focus.

Chapter 17

"Believe in your heart that you're meant to live a life full of passion, purpose, magic and miracles."
~ *Roy T. Bennett, The Light in the Heart*

Arabella opened her eyes and instinctively knew it had to be close to dawn even though her bedroom was still relatively dark. She looked over at the clock. The bright red numbers said five-thirty in the morning. More sleep her body begged. She and Alberto had been up off and on all night making love, talking, laughing, falling asleep, waking up again and repeating the cycle. She was tired, ached in new places, and still she felt alive.

Why didn't my alarm go off? What day is it? Saturday? Please let it be Saturday she thought. Quick remnants of her work week flashed through her haze. It had to be Saturday. No alarm is set for Saturday mornings. All the other days, she had obligations and commitments to be up and out. Last night, she'd been free to indulge herself with Alberto, the masterful lover who made her body hum like an instrument. Even now with her back to him, she could feel the warmth emanating from his powerful body. Was he still asleep? She stopped thinking to listen. She heard his gentle breathing, in...out...in...out. Yes, he was asleep.

Arabella dare not move and wake him as she knew from their brief affair he was a light sleeper. As a matter of fact, he rarely slept, always getting up in the early morning hours to work in the fields and production facilities. If he wasn't in one of those places, he'd be in the office funneling through reports and paperwork which often lasted into the late hours. She could not fathom how he kept up that pace. She had always labeled herself a workaholic, and he even surpassed her.

She remembered back to when she first arrived in Spain. She'd paid attention to everyone's schedule as she'd learned about the nuances of the business. Considering the conditions to which the company had hired her, she thought Alberto was only working long hours to irritate her. Now she knew better. They both loved their work and seeing miracles be produced. While they had different methods, he was just as demanding on himself as she was on herself; both of them committed to delivering excellence and providing assistance wherever needed. Halfway around the world, who knew there was a male version of her! A scary thought indeed that had materialized as Alberto Gutiérrez! However, here in Jaén with this man, she was so out of her league in a high stakes game. His fire was consuming her thoughts a little too often for her level of comfort.

For the good of the company, and all the bystanders, they'd been civil in public, only disagreed in private and now worked together on most issues. Even though she was technically his boss, they'd created a tense partnership from day one (or at least sometime in that first week once he realized she was not leaving or backing down). They mutually respected each other's domain. She left the farming to him and he stepped aside to watch as she trained the workers to implement her extraction technology. When training was done, she'd return back to the office.

If Alberto disagreed with her, he never did so in front of anyone else, and he always asked his skeptical questions in private. Only a few times had they got into a shouting match that others might overhear. Most knew if Alberto was on the warpath it was best to get out of his way or make oneself scarce. Arabella refused to back down, even if he wanted her to give in. Her mom always told her, "no point coming to play in a man's world if you are going to ask permission. Make no excuses, do your best and get the job done!"

She certainly was not like many of the women she'd watched capitulate to a dominant male's point of view or defer to a man to make a decision. It was still a mystery how she and Alberto got here, laying side by side. Neither of them pretended they had the power to dominate the other, even if they wanted to. She was captain of her own vessel, ruler of her own kingdom. No man was going to boss her around or win. That is, with the exception of her brother who was bossy in a protective sort of way. Most of the time she allowed Alejandro a little more latitude.

Arabella did not consider Alberto to ever be like a brother to her. From day one she felt he was too damn sexy and always nearby. It unnerved her to see the sweat glisten off his brow and other places when he helped the workers. In the field, he usually had on a simple white T-shirt and jeans; in the office, an open collar buttoned down cotton shirt, slacks, and no tie. No matter what he wore, his broad shoulders, muscled chest and sculptured shape easily forced his clothes to meld to his skin. It also forced her thoughts to meander in ways that could in no way be considered office appropriate.

After they fell into bed on the night of the ball, Arabella had no intention of having an "affair" to last. It was a "one night only" adventure. Damn if he wasn't a lady killer in a tuxedo, all the rough work edges washed away. He'd offered her a ride home—he'd waited for her patiently, even when business beckoned her to finish saying goodbye to clients. She felt taken care of with no promise of anything else. He'd been so different as he made love to her that night; almost reverent to her needs and putting her first. He shared his passion, never taking his pleasure before she was satisfied. That threw her for a loop. He seemed so hot-headed in the office and determined to have his way. Maybe she'd wrongly judged him? A few nights didn't seem like enough to get to know the real man under the facade of work. He was a hard worker, happy to do manual labor and get dirty. He could be stuck in his viewpoint, at least in the beginning. He was also well educated, and yet down to earth. So many contrasts.

To this day, neither of them knew what to do with their lust for one another. After that first weekend of love making, they'd agreed to keep work strictly professional and not divulge to anyone they'd slept together. It was only meant to be that one lapse in common sense. Clearly they'd failed to keep that agreement. Numerous times. Pretending to be enemies who'd declared an uneasy truce when others were around was getting more and more difficult. On rare occasions when they were out in public for dinner, they'd mostly talked business, with innuendo thrown in for good measure. Alberto always started the teasing and raised it to a level of almost seduction. He made it hard to concentrate. Prior to taking this position, she'd always held herself in tight control, unwilling to mix business and pleasure. Not anymore. He was teaching her how to act on her desires in new ways even if she didn't want to admit it. She was teaching him what it was like to have met your match. And they were well matched, at least for now.

Go back to sleep, the voice from her brain said. Oh right she'd been thinking way too much! She closed her eyes and silently listened again to the sounds around her, relaxing her mind, controlling her breathing. Then she heard it—a downpour of rain outside pelting the roof. It was as if the skies had opened up and the waterfall was drenching life. Where had that soaking come from? Was it supposed to be raining today? Why'd it have to be today? She sighed. So much for her idea of going into the mountain groves today. It was a late fall Saturday and she didn't want to spend her day in the office.

"You're awake," she heard Alberto's raspy morning voice next to her.

Ugh! No denying it, he too was now awake. She turned herself over to face him. There he lay on his side looking sexy as all hell with tousled curls, and sleepy eyes. "Mmhmmm, I am. Sorry to wake you." Her voice sounded a bit raspy too.

She watched his lips curve into the most delicious smile she had ever seen. "Good morning la meva bella. You have nothing to apologize for. I love being awakened by you." With that pronouncement, he leaned over and gently kissed her cheek.

Alas, even though her nickname was Bella, she liked being called 'his beautiful.' And that kiss was so genteel.

"Thank you!" She demurely responded to him. He was pure charmer when he wanted to be. She knew the passion he pretended didn't exist behind that restful look. His blood boiled red hot when sparked, both in and out of bed. Oh the way he's looking at me is so alluring. She was fighting hard not to move in closer, put her lips on his. As if they hadn't made love all night, her body still craved to have him again. She closed her eyes. Best to steer this awakening in a productive direction. Deep breath. When she opened her eyes again, he was staring back at her. She could tell he was searching to get a read on her mood.

"What's wrong Bella?"

It was as if he could sense her pulling away. She cleared her throat unbending in her resolve. "It's raining. Pretty hard it sounds like."

He stopped to listen. "Si, now I hear it. It is a good thing to have rain so the lands grow, is it not?

She pondered the words delivered in a thick accent. She had to agree with his assessment. "Yes it is."

"So what's troubling you so early on this new day?"

"The rain. It's not convenient to our plans. Remember last night you said you'd take me through the back fields today."

"I said a lot of things last night." He smiled that smile again.

She immediately blushed remembering all the words he'd whispered to her in English and Spanish while they'd flirted their way through dinner, indulged in foreplay in the car, and haphazardly fell into her bed to release all their pent up desires. She tilted her head. "Yes and I guess the field trip will have to wait."

"The fields are not going anywhere querida! There will be many opportunities to go explore and discover."

She smiled letting go of the sense of urgency. He was right yet again and she wasn't going to put it into words. Instead, she moved the topic in another direction. "So tell me, what does one do around here on a rainy day?"

"You mean on a day when there is no work to do?" He laughed heartily. "When would that ever be the case querida? There's always work to do."

She rolled her eyes. "I'm being serious Alberto!"

"Si, okay. Please let me think." He rubbed his chin with his hand, looking pensive.

She waited. Silence.

"Well," he said finally speaking with a spark in his eyes. "We could stay in bed and make love all day." He put his arm over her waist and scooped her closer as if she weighed nothing.

That was the last thing she wanted to do. Who was she kidding? She'd love to. And, she knew she needed to level out the playing field. When she was in bed with him he had the upper hand, even if she was unwilling to admit to that either! Most days she was no match for her desire to be with him. She was not giving in to her base desires. Not this time!

"As inviting as that sounds, no. We are getting up now," she said as she placed his hand back over to his hip and moved out of his embrace. She turned onto her back and sprang upright. As she went to get out of the bed, she pulled the sheet with her and wrapped it around her naked frame. It had been their only cover. That left Alberto in all his naked glory still in the bed. She did not let her eyes roam beyond his eyes. And then she turned and sauntered away.

"Fine! I'm getting up," she heard him say as she walked into the bathroom to take her shower. Alone!

******

As the bedroom door opened, Arabella looked up from the mirror where she'd been brushing her newly dried hair. Alberto strolled in, announcing, "I have an idea of something we can do!"

Even though he spoke in a serious and focused tone, he'd obviously just emerged from the shower. His wet hair glistened and all he wore was a towel wrapped tightly around his torso. Who needed to look at oneself in the mirror when they could gaze upon him instead? Arabella turned herself around in the vanity chair, all eyes now fully on him.

"You've come up with something other than staying in bed?" She said in disbelief as she let her eyes finally rest on his. She could see the amusement over there as she fought to concentrate on the words he was saying, not on his body that constantly captivated her curiosity.

"Yes, I did! Let's go into Granada and be tourists for a day! Have you ever been to the Alahambra?"

"Okay!" She said considering the request. "And to answer your question, no I have never been there. I wanted to go and was not able to get a ticket on my first weekend here in Spain. They told me tickets are booked up months in advance."

"That is often the case. It is a beautiful place and visitors come to the Andalusia region because it is priority stop on their tours."

"How will we get in if it is already booked?"

"No worries, I have a friend who oversees the facility. I called him and it has been arranged."

She tentatively answered, "Sure, then we can go." She turned her head slightly to look out the now opened curtains of the nearby window. Then confirming for herself what daylight held, she turned back to him. "You do know it's still raining, right? We'll get soaked? Will it even be open?"

"Si! The Alahambra is rarely ever closed. It will be all the better for us on a rainy day. The crowds are smaller. Plus, most of the paths are concrete. Even though it is still relatively warm and rain is not predicted to last, I would recommend you wear your rain boots. With any luck, the rain will stop. We can't visit the mountain groves today as I promised. It is too wet to be on those roads. I won't risk an accident."

She was immediately excited and giddy with the idea of seeing the Alahambra. "We can play in the rain as tourists! That will be fun! I'm almost ready to go. Maybe you could go get dressed now? You in a towel is quite distracting."

"No worries querida! We now have plans for our day, and I am not going to let you seduce me out of following through on them!" He laughed, dropped his towel and disappeared into the closet.

"That was so wrong Alberto!" She said to the posterior side of his naked figure. Arabella promised herself she'd pay him back. He simply kept laughing.

Chapter 18

"My object is merely to give the reader a general introduction into an abode where, if so disposed, he may linger and loiter with me day by day until we gradually become familiar with all its localities."
~ Washington Irving, Tales of the Alhambra

Alberto opened the car door and Arabella stepped out. The Alahambra complex faced her. They were officially in Andalusia, in a massive complex hidden on this side amongst the trees as it sat atop Granada's grand cityscape. She was dressed in practical clothing: jeans, sweater, rain jacket and boots as Alberto had suggested. Even though the rain had slowed to a drizzle, the dim skies promised more showers to come, and it was soggy wet everywhere she looked. He held open a giant clear umbrella big enough to cover them both from the falling mist. Her hair would be frizzy in a matter of minutes. Oh well, a worthwhile price to pay for adventure. This was going to be a fun day after all!

As they moved along the path Arabella could see more buildings—good shelter from possible downpours to come. The complex was bigger than she'd originally imagined. Alberto paused them under the overhang just before the main gate. "Wait here a second while I go get our tickets."

"Not going anywhere. I promise!"

He promptly secured their passes from the window and walked her through the entry gates onto the property. She turned to take in the setting. She was finally here, at the magical place she'd seen from her hotel room and heard was a must-see all those months ago.

Just beyond the portico he spoke, "Welcome to the Alahambra, known as the Red Fortress. Wait till you see the intricacies inside!"

They were on top of the world as if on a cliff. It was as if the place was designed as a lookout point to announce whomever considered themselves worthy to ascend and greet royalty. "This place already looks beautiful, very serene. What do you know of its history?"

"I remember a little from civics class in school. Many important events happened here. Would you like to take the formal tour?"

Arabella thought to herself. She wasn't in the mood to hear a bunch of history facts. It was too romantic and charming in the rain to pay attention to some scholar drone on and expect her full attention. Maybe it was being with Alberto that was distracting. She realized she had not answered his question and said, "No thank you. Perhaps another time. I'd much rather you fill me in on your version?"

"But of course. I will do my best. Worst case there is the internet if I get stumped. We have all-access passes so no one will bother us and we are free to meander around as long as you want."

"We'll be exhausted when we're done."

"Yes. I'm sure we'll be hungry too. Afterwards, we can get a meal in town down below if you'd like. And if we're too tired to return to Jaén, we can always spend the night here in Granada. My treat!"

"Thank you! That plan sounds perfect!" No Alberto was perfect. She loved that he thought ahead. This morning she'd just jumped up and said let's go. Details were minuscule annoyances when she wasn't working or conducting research. He always seemed to scan the environment taking care of things, taking care of her. Strangely enough she never thought she'd like a man to take care of her needs, and she did. Perhaps too much so with Alberto.

"Excellent, let the tour commence," she heard him say as he reached down to take her hand in his.

A warm sizzle coursed through her veins. Yes, today would be memorable. "Where do we start?"

"We'll begin in the Nasrid Palaces, and then go through the gardens. We'll end our exploration in the Generalife area, also known as the summer palace. There's lots of ground to cover. Let's see what I remember of history as we go along." He laughed, clearly finding humor that his memory might not be the best. She smiled without responding, already convinced he'd remember more than he thought he would. His mind was too sharp and attuned to his surroundings not to remember.

"The Alahambra is a fortified palace that has held many treasures and housed kings and queens. It is said to be a pearl set amidst emeralds because of the white washed walls and its location in a forest of green English elms."

"Then why have they also called it the 'Red Fortress'?"

"Ah Si. Alahambra in Arabic means red. The original foundation was made from red clay and so the name was chosen. Construction began in the 9th Century by the emir which is the Muslim title for military commander. The Emirate of Granada was ruled from these very walls. Over the centuries more buildings were added to the complex, but the structure was dramatically renovated in the 1300s and inside rooms were added during different periods. The last Muslim dynasty on the Iberian Peninsula ended when the Catholics took control in 1492. What remains is an amazing display of artistic creativity hidden in the hills. Did you know this place is on the UNESCO World Heritage list?"

She shook her head no. As old as it is, it would make sense though to be on that list. He had a good memory for the facts. And already she noticed she didn't care what Alberto was saying per se. She was mesmerized by his strong masculine hand holding her smaller one, and his thick accent speaking of a fairy tale place she'd not even known had existed before her arrival in Spain. Focus, focus, focus!

They followed the walkway and entered the upper building of the Nasrid Palaces. Almost immediately she could see the inside was ornately carved with stunning plasterwork. It was crafted with intricate patterns and designs. Aligned and carefully complimenting the areas surrounding doorways, arches and corners. "The windows and entrances are so detailed, yet elegant."

"Si. It is said that while much of the complex has Moor influences, it also has Christian and Renaissance ones too. The palaces were separated into three sections of rooms: some for administrators, others to handle affairs of state and then of course the harem. In 1492, King Ferdinand and Queen Isabella made the Alhambra a central part of their Royal Court. Spain has taken a concerted effort to restore and preserve this place over these last centuries. Now that it is a national historical site, we receive expertise in archaeology and restoration from all over the world."

They continued to stroll in silence for a while. She moved closer to the walls in some rooms to see if the plaster was real. When she could no longer stay quiet, she said, "I cannot describe how exquisite it is here. The amount of care they took to complement each segment, it's like it tells a story."

"That is exactly the intention. The tiled walls are said to be mathematical works of art. Others say the patterns are a type of themed wallpaper to celebrate the purpose of a room. We'll likely never know the real answer as much the information was never formally passed down."

"We haven't gone very far and I'm so impressed."

"Wait until you see the Courtyard of the Lions. There is a fountained water garden there. Come, I will show you."

She followed him along until they reached a breathtaking scene that unfolded at the center of everything. "Wow."

"This rectangle shaped courtyard is set amid one hundred twenty-four marble columns, and it's is the center of the harem. You see the fountain? It's surrounded by twelve marble lions in the middle. One lion for each sign of the zodiac. It is said this courtyard was the central location for family life." He pointed downward. "Do you see the marble flooring?"

"Yes," she said as her eyes followed his hand.

"If you look along the lines from the center, you'll notice it makes way for water to flow from there into the surrounding halls and back again to the central basin. I can't remember any other details as to what it symbolizes."

"That's plenty. It flows like running water through a faucet. Yet its completion predates such an invention centuries later. I want to look at the carved walls, columns and faces of the lions. Yet the water flow has me want to follow its path."

"Yes. Every time I come here, I see something new. I know whatever the detail, it was here all the other times, and I just missed it."

She twirled around in a slow circle as she observed the scene, including the misty rain falling across the open courtyard. "I'd like to come back here one sunny day and see how the pattern of the sun falls across this space."

When she'd stopped to face the fountain once more, he turned to her and pulled her into his arms. His eagle eyes looked into hers, piercing her soul. "You have my word querida. I will bring you here again one sunny day."

He leaned in to kiss her right there at the edge of the courtyard. She was not used to being on display in public, and she didn't care. She wove her hands around his neck. The promise of more to come was on his lips. She was breathless when he stopped kissing her. He said nothing more for many minutes as they struggled to return their breathing to normal. Then he took her hand again and pulled her gently along into a set of new rooms as if nothing ever happened.

After many turns, he spoke once more. "This is the Comares Tower. It is said that this was the place where the turnover of Granada was decided." They walked along a little further. "And this room might be of more interest than just its spectacular architecture. This is the Hall of the Ambassadors. Legend has it, this is the room in which Christopher Columbus was commissioned to go find the 'new' world. Queen Isabella was instrumental in the consideration of Columbus' request to expand the Royal Court's interests. From here with the king and queen's blessings and resources Columbus set off and discovered the Americas."

She stopped to look at him. "In this very room? Over five hundred years ago?"

"Si querida. Time has moved along, yet a fortress has survived even as history spanned through many eras and rulers. Lest we should forget, lives were made and destroyed in these ruins. Our current generation pays little attention to plaster, brick and mortar in this technological age."

"I wonder what the generations will say about us in future centuries."

"That we kept these old relics around for no reason?"

She giggled. "Yes by then we'll have a lot more output thought to be the technological marvels of their time. I suspect it will all have become just another relic!"

"I'm sure. And these buildings will still be here too. Anyway, it's not raining very much, so let's walk through the gardens and then to the summer palace."

They meandered through formal gardens filled with every kind of flower, fountain and pool—all meant to draw one's attention into the sheer beauty of a truly royal place. The views of the mountains and caves in the distance were surreal—they looked out windows to the world. Arabella was swayed by the aroma of rich blooms only slightly dampened with the rain. Lavender fields, rows of roses, and orange trees planted along the building edges were just some of the foliage she'd noticed. By the time they'd walked up the 'Hill of the Sun' and onto the Generalife Summer Palace grounds with more terraces, fountains and paths, Arabella was exhausted and hungry. They strolled around for another fifteen minutes taking in the playful scene of water amidst lush greenery. She was getting dizzy and needed to sit down soon or else she might pass out. Chocolate croissants for breakfast hadn't been enough to last. . .

"I love it here. But would you mind if we headed into town for a meal soon though? I'm actually starving."

"Not at all. We've been walking around for a long time. I'd say it's definitely time for lunch! We can see what we missed on our next visit."

"Oh that's wonderful news. Thanks for bringing me here."

"You're most welcome Bella Bella! Come, I know a shortcut back to the car. And a great place for lunch." He wrapped his arm around her and walked her back to his vehicle.

She was beyond happy! And super glad she'd get to sit down and also eat soon!

******

He drove them a short distance to a restaurant called Carmen de Aben Humeya. Another beautiful place—quaint and understated with romantic ambiance, and large floor to ceiling glass windows that held amazing views of the Alahambra. It had stopped raining finally and the waiter sat them at a corner table by the windows. The view was spectacular on an overcast day. They could've sat out on the balcony and didn't want to chance the rain was truly over. It was around two in the afternoon, and the establishment was not overly crowded. That was good news for her grumbling stomach.

Alberto ordered for them and she was grateful when the first small plate appetizers arrived within minutes. A simple plate of melon served with razor thin ham, a basket of bread, and bowl of sautéed peas.

Arabella drizzled olive oil onto the bread and placed the ham on top. It probably was not the intended design for consumption and she didn't care. "I'm famished," she said picking up her makeshift open faced sandwich.

"Me too," He said looking across at her.

She literally had the piece of bread halfway to her mouth as he'd spoken. Oh, he's not talking about food. A haze of desire swept over her. She gently set the food down, closed her eyes and took a full breath. He couldn't be serious. When she blinked them open again, his expression was no different. "Alberto, please! Might we make it through this meal so we fortify our bodies and have the energy to make love?"

"You are so practical! Alright. I will succumb to your request. At least for now." He spread his hands into an open gesture. "Let's eat."

No sooner had he said those words, she picked up the ham and bread from the plate and bit into it. Divine. She didn't stop until all of it was gone. While Alberto might have pretended he wasn't hungry for food, he had no problem consuming his portion as well. They made small talk about nothing in particular. Other dishes came from the kitchen. Mozzarella and tomato salad, roast duck and sautéed potatoes, fried eggplant. At some point, Arabella lifted her white napkin and waved it. "No mas! It was all delicious food. And I'm stuffed."

"Si. I think that was the point. My parents are good friends with the owner. We always overeat here."

"Well I felt like we went from being starving paupers to royalty."

Alberto smirked. "Would you like dessert, querida?"

She wasn't walking into his trap. "You mean more food? No thank you. Coffee though would be lovely. "

"Very well." He called the waiter over and requested only coffee.

While they sipped on the after meal drinks, she wondered what they would do next. Daylight would soon be gone now that the days were getting shorter.

He spoke cutting into her thoughts. "Do you want to stay over here in Granada or head back to the estate?"

"It really is up to you as you're the driver."

"I'm fine either way."

"If we're going to end up back in bed, and I hope we will, we might as well go back to my place. That way in the morning we are close enough to do our paperwork for the week ahead."

"You talk about how much I work. Now you're the one cutting into our down time."

"You do work too much! I'm not going to turn our fun day into unhappy ending spawned by a debate."

"What are you saying querida? You don't want to hear my opinion on the subject?"

She smiled, knowing she was about to win this round. "Alberto, I like it here in Granada and you promised we will come back. Maybe we can plan it out and stay over for a weekend soon. And right this moment, I'm ready to go home. Are you going to take me to bed so I can pay you back with my body for teasing me this morning? Or do I need to find my own ride home, alone?"

She could see Alberto's expression change across the table. He got the message. He put his hand up and signaled for the check without saying another word. They were headed back to Jaén, and this perfect day would end as it had started...in bed with Alberto.

Chapter 19

"Scientists have become the bearers of the torch of discovery in our quest for knowledge."
~ Stephen Hawking

"What is it, Jose?"

"Juan Carlos is here to see you?"

Arabella frowned. What could Juan Carlos want? "Okay, send him in."

Arabella rose from her desk and went to stand in front of it. She was about to greet the Chairman of the Board and Alberto's brother.

"Dr. Gomez, thanks for agreeing to see me." He firmly shook her offered hand.

"Of course. Please have a seat. And call me Arabella."

"Yes, Arabella. I'm sorry to disturb your work." He sat down in the seat nearest her desk. She chose to sit in the chair across from him, versus returning to the other side of the desk.

"It is never a bother. I owe you a great deal for championing my work and for all the support. Now what can I do for you?"

"I appreciate how direct you are. So I'll get to the reason I'm here. I just left a marketing meeting about our American interests and expanding our distribution."

"That sounds promising."

"It is. And I have a request."

"Oh?" For the life of her she couldn't imagine what that request might be. She kept her smile in place while she waited for him to say more.

"Yes. If it wouldn't be too much of an inconvenience, we'd like to leverage your skills and heritage."

Arabella was leery now. "How so? I am just a scientist and have no skills to market anything. In my estimation, either people want something and buy it or they don't."

"It is true you are a scientist, si? What's not true is you saying you have no marketing skills. You've done an amazing job marketing your automated approach to extract the olives. You've come here sight unseen and convinced everyone to try something new. And they're doing it."

"Well not everyone!"

Juan Carlos laughed. "Si! My brother, how do you say it in your country...is a tough cookie?"

Arabella laughed too. "Yes that's the expression."

"He'll come around. Anyway, we could benefit from having someone inside our company who is from America to help us expand our sales there."

Juan Carlos was all business, and she liked that. No niceties or fake accolades. She had no interest in the idea even though she was grateful to be holding her position. Surely there was a better way. "How about hiring an American marketing company?"

"We tried that first! We've hired several companies over the last couple of years. It didn't get us one single additional contract beyond where we'd already made inroads."

"Oh! Well I don't know much about sales or distribution for olive oil."

"That is true. And yet with your knowledge of the growing process, extraction, pressing, and oil quality—you are in a unique position to answer any questions and allay doubts. In talking with you, they'd trust your reputation and be willing to give us a shot. The quality of the products would take care of the rest. Plus, you grew up in wine country and understand American food preferences."

Ummmmm. Arabella didn't know what to say. She does have expertise in those areas.

Juan Carlos must have heard her apprehension for he replied, "We wouldn't ask or interrupt your work if we thought there was any other way."

She was wavering. "Okay. What does helping entail?" Like a dog with a bone, he was determined to have his plan happen. So she'd do well to try to help if she could to keep an ally in her corner.

"A couple of trips to conferences for a few days each time. Specifically New York first and then maybe California. You could visit home. We'll get you a calendar of possible events. We don't want this to interfere with your other important activities."

They weren't asking for much. She could do a couple short trips. "I would be willing to help out."

"Excellente! One more detail. Mama thought it was a good idea for Alberto to go too."

"What?" This sounded like a disaster.

"He is one of the faces of our family. He also has the authority to begin negotiations and set up the next actions we'll take from here in Jaén."

Arabella didn't know how she felt about travelling with Alberto. No one knew about their affair. She wasn't sure about any of this. So she'd have to tread carefully with her words. "Alberto and I don't exactly agree on much."

"Yes, I know he can be stubborn and difficult, but he always puts the company's well-being before his ego. I promise he'll be on his best behavior."

Arabella had already agreed to go. She couldn't back out now. "We'll see if that is true. I'll hold you to that promise."

"Deal. And thank you! We'll owe you for doing this Arabella! Now I'll let you get back to work while I go break the news to my brother."

She decided it best not to react to what Alberto's reaction might be. "It'll all be worth it. Thanks for stopping by Juan Carlos. I'll look forward to the details."

With that he stood up and went to the door. "Hasta Luego."

Arabella stayed in her seat, already caught up in how she got herself in this mess. The lines between business and pleasure were getting more blurry by the day. "Si hasta luego." I am not in a relationship with Alberto; it is just an affair!

******

That evening as she was sitting on the porch, Alberto pulled up unexpectedly. She suspected he was coming to discuss their new and impending trip.

"Hi Bella Bella!" He approached the porch and came over to kiss her briefly on the lips.

"Alberto. Did you hear the news?" She was in no mood to make small talk.

"Yep! You okay with it?" He asked as he sat down next to her on the rattan chair.

"Your brother is very persuasive. I'll convince myself to be okay with it."

"Yeah you didn't have a choice either, huh?"

"Nope at the point he mentioned your mother, I was stuck."

"We'll make the best of it."

"Yes we will. In the meantime, come give me a proper kiss."

"Your wish is my command." He came over and pulled her up into his embrace. He leaned in and their lips met.

If nothing else, she was distracted now and being with him was the best end to a difficult and demanding day.

Chapter 20

"A journey is like marriage. The certain way to be wrong is to think you control it."
~ John Steinbeck

The plane landed just about 1 o'clock in the afternoon at New York City's John F. Kennedy International Airport, also affectionately known as JFK. It was going to be a quick trip for a two-day olive oil industry conference. Arabella has been a member for years and had been to this particular conference many times. The Board recommended she take her nemesis, Alberto. He could use some time away, and to meet the "who's who," they'd said. He was not happy they were sending him when he considered being in the fields more important. She didn't argue with him the point of view. Since Alberto had become her lover too, she was conflicted with how to keep her work and home lives separate. They were always together. From early morning till late at night. This trip was designed for them to research ways to target east coast scientific interests in what Gutiérrez Enterprises considered prime-time exposure. Arabella had suggested the Board send someone else in the company or just send Alberto. After all, she'd only been with the company for a few months. The Board simply said the decision was made and she was the best option. She'd accepted her fate. Plus there could always be worse places to go than New York City!

"Ready to take on the world, querida?"

"As ready as I'm going to get," she said as she picked up her purse and deplaned with Alberto.

"The sooner we start, the sooner we'll be done and can return home to Jaen."

"Agreed!" And so their official work trip began.

******

It was finally Friday! Alberto sat across from her as they watched people come and go in the lobby bar of the famed NYC Marquis Hotel while awaiting a hired car to take them back to JFK airport. There they'd catch the company jet and return to Spain. Arabella was grateful their planned itinerary would get them into Granada-Jaén airport around midnight and she'd get to sleep in her own bed. If she was lucky, he'd stay the night with her too.

She picked up her glass to suggest a toast to their return to Jaén just as his cell phone rang to interrupt. She looked up into his face just in time to see him frown down at the phone. He picked it up, answering in Spanish. And while she was unsure of what would make him grimace, she had no desire to eavesdrop on his call. Instead, she turned slightly in her seat to stare across the open space and sip from her champagne cocktail. She'd never been a fan of alcohol early in the day. However, it was apropos to meet up and celebrate a job well done before going back to their "real" jobs. Champagne and snacks were a respectable choice no matter the hour. The sparkling drink mixed with cranberry juice was especially tasty.

While she awaited his call to end, Arabella also gave herself permission to think back over these last few days. Overall it was a successful trip. They'd secured a couple of new deals and she'd gotten to spend time with Alberto out of his element here on neutral turf. Days that included meeting after meeting with little time to catch her breath or sightsee in the Big Apple. Even though they were both scientists, master chemists one might say—she and Alberto had a good handle on the business side of the enterprise. Juan Carlos was right about her being able to allay concerns, speak to oil quality and gain trust. When each day was done, they'd compile their notes during working dinners. They said the same things just in different ways, worked well together and always used the time to improve upon the previous presentation. They'd even addressed all the questions that came forward. While Alberto had full authority to negotiate the final terms, he'd decided to leave it to his brothers to talk sales and numbers. He'd chuckled telling her it was his way of creating work for them while he caught up on his over the weekend.

Before their arrival in New York, they'd agreed it would be wise to remain professional in case someone saw them. Maybe it wasn't quite agreement; she'd demanded it and he'd complied. Being romantic partners on official business trips might decrease their credibility—hers being something she'd worked too hard to establish. Each night Arabella suppressed the urge to invite Alberto into her bed, and it took a lot of determined grit to return to her own room alone. He'd been the perfect gentleman and they were all business, at least most of the time. There was the one evening they'd gone for a late dinner and he'd convinced her to take a horse drawn carriage ride in Central Park. She'd never been on one—it wasn't the kind of thing people from California were into doing. If you wanted to ride a horse, you went to the stables, selected yours and went riding. She said yes to a new experience. That's funny! Being with Alberto was always new. On the ride with the light of a full moon, they sat close and held hands under the lightweight blanket. The horse and its master traipsed around the legendary NYC Park. At some point she'd gazed up into Alberto's eyes and he kissed her. She didn't care who might be watching. She wanted that kiss to never end as if she was a love struck groupie.

Alberto hadn't made it any better when he abruptly stopped and then whispered in her ear, "Querida, it will take everything I have not to take you to my bed right now." She forced herself to come back to reality, still in the lobby and unwilling to relive another second of that night. It was best to avoid being hot and bothered yet again in public. Shaking her head slightly, she realized Alberto was still on the phone.

"Si, she's right here. We're just about to leave for the airport. Si, si I will tell her. I'm sure she'll understand." She turned back around in her seat and set the half empty glass down. He saw her look at him. "Gracias. Adios!" He pressed a button and ended the call.

She continued to make eye contact and stopped pretending she wasn't listening or hadn't heard the very end of his call. "Tell me what? Is your mother okay?" she said leading him to answer her exact questions instead of waiting a moment longer.

"That was Juan Carlos. And si, Mama is good. We've just been requested to go to California versus back to Spain."

"What? Why?"

"Our representative, Dante—who was going to California's Wine & Olive Oil Festival tomorrow through Sunday—has appendicitis and is being rushed into surgery."

She put her hand to her mouth in shock. "Oh goodness, is he okay?"

"Yes. He'd been complaining of stomach pain while in the office. They sent him to the nurse. She was able to assess his symptoms and recommend he go to the emergency room. They took some tests and diagnosed his acute condition. It is a good thing he didn't get on that plane. His appendix could have ruptured in midair."

"He's very lucky," she said thinking of all the possible ways that Dante might have been in medical trouble while on travel.

Alberto shrugged. "Si. Not so much us though? We must extend our trip until Monday. There is a display to inspect and a couple meetings to attend. Bertram has filed a new flight plan. Juan Carlos said to buy whatever clothes and expenses you need and the company will cover it."

"That won't be necessary, I always over pack. What part of California?" she asked as if she didn't know.

"It's in the San Francisco area, maybe somewhere near Napa. Aren't you from around that region?"

Arabella was heating up very fast. Unsure of whether it was the champagne or her nerves at this point. She answered quietly, "yes."

"Good. At least you'll get to go home for a few days. My brother, knowing how much we both like to work, sends his deepest apologies. He hopes you'll at least enjoy being back in California though. He was unsure how close the festival is to your hometown, and whether you still kept your abode. So he had the travel folks set us up two hotel rooms versus just getting me one and you staying at your place."

"It's fine. Medical emergencies can't be avoided. A few more days away won't harm anything and we're technically still connected to the staff if they need something. Oh! I'd much prefer the hotel as this is a business trip!" Arabella didn't want to talk about home, go to her place or even think about seeing anyone she knew. Especially not her brother, Alejandro. Hiding her relationship with Alberto was hard enough around strangers who didn't care one way or another. Her brother was a whole new entity when it came down to protecting her interests. Alejandro had a way of interpreting what was best for her.

Her affair with Alberto was just that right now—they enjoyed each other's company and there was no easy way to explain that to her brother. She was grown and didn't need him to inspect her romantic affairs. Who was she kidding? He'd put his opinion in no matter what. She'd just have to avoid Alejandro for two days. How hard could it be? Maybe he was out of town or too busy to attend the festival. Or so she'd hope really hard. Maybe fate was on her side this one time...

Alberto interrupted her panic attack. "Our car has arrived. We'll get our travel details on the plane. If you're ready, I'll settle up the bill and we can go."

"Yes!" she answered lying through her teeth. She hated not being truthful with him. Truth was she was never going to be ready to take this trek. And she wasn't in a mood to spoil their celebration. At least not yet.

******

Arabella sat brushing her hair, preparing for the day. This was the last day of the festival, and they could relax a little. The subcontractor they'd hired to set up and manage the display was receiving good feedback. Their meetings, while not as promising as those in New York, still left them open to expanding their American portfolio. So far, another good trip.

She and Alberto had arrived in the San Francisco Bay Area that Friday afternoon. They'd picked up the rental car and leisurely enjoyed the drive down from San Jose airport. It was a smaller airport with less commercial traffic; instead it caters to those who could afford the private and chartered jet experiences. Arabella didn't mind so much being with the snobby, exclusive folks as she hated large crowds of people. People who pushed into you or pretended they didn't see you were the worst. She missed Jaén where the people were real, polite and unpretentious.

Alberto walked through the door of the adjoining hotel room to interrupt her musings. "You almost ready to go?"

She wasn't. "I need five more minutes."

"Buenas." He came over and leaned down to kiss her on the lips. "Meet in the lobby in ten?"

"Yes," she said breathlessly.

She watched him turn, walk back through the same door he'd come from moments before and close it behind him. They'd not requested to be in connected rooms, and she was grateful to discover their good fortune after check in. Being with his easy going morning routine and desire to stay on schedule was comforting. She liked other things about him too. Like how he made love to her last night, slow and steady with no suppressed emotions—just the two of them behind closed doors like back in Spain. Always when sleeping in the same bed, they could reunite to satiate their desires and cuddle—she loved falling asleep that way. For two nights no one from the outside knew, and she was free to have it all or some semblance of having it all. When it was time for them to leave each day, they closed the doors back and left separately. While no one likely cared what they did or didn't do, people were always watching and she couldn't jeopardize her position. One more day and then back home where they could go back to normal! She put the brush down saying aloud, "Time to get on with it."

They met in the lobby. "Do you want to drive?" He said as they walked to the valet desk.

"No, not today. I'm feeling a little tired." Tired was not the right word. She was exhausted. They'd barely slept last night. She didn't know how Alberto did it. Work, little sleep and then coming to make love with her too.

"Oh? Too much work?" He smiled.

She lowered her voice for fear of being overheard. "Don't play Mr. Innocent. You know why I'm tired."

With a wide smile and slight bow, he said "Madame, I have no idea what you're talking about. And I'm at your service anytime you want."

She opened her mouth to say something and didn't get a chance to respond. Alberto had turned his attention to the valet pulling up in their car. The young man jumped out to hand off the keys to Alberto, who took them with command and authority and provided a tip for service rendered. Alberto then opened the car's passenger door and she got in. How'd he do that? Make sure everything was taken care of with smooth efficiency?

Once in the vehicle himself, he turned out of the complex in the direction of the festival. The facade of all business was back in place. As they arrived at the festival, Arabella could see it was already very crowded. She knew it would be like this on the last day with beautiful weather too. She hated the thought of being bumped along and fighting to see. Crowds were good for business and a sure sign the festival is a hit.

"What's wrong querida?" He must have seen her hesitate.

"Nothing. I just don't like big crowds. It makes me anxious like the world is closing in on me."

"What can I do to make it better? I will go alone and you can take the car. Perhaps a day at the spa would be preferable?"

"Thank you and no. This is my job, so I'll adjust."

"You sure? It has been a long week and you do need some rest."

"No, I'll be fine. It might just take a few extra minutes."

"I promise I will be there every step of the way."

"You won't lose me on purpose?" she said trying to smile and finding humor also calmed her nerves.

"Bella Bella, no way in hell would I lose you! I am here by your side. If it gets too difficult, we'll leave together, si?"

She was joking and he wasn't buying her attempt to change the dynamic. "Yes, si."

"Please take two deep breaths and then we'll go. Together!"

No point in arguing. He'd offered her a compromise. Go together, make the best of it, and leave together. So she did as he'd asked. Surprisingly the deep breaths and his promise did provide her a sense of comfort. "I'm ready!"

Chapter 21

"Love is like an earthquake - unpredictable, a little scary, but when the hard part is over you realize how lucky you truly are." ~ James Earl Jones

"Bella, is that you?"

Arabella heard the voice calling her by the nickname only few people knew. Her nerves immediately went into overdrive again and her heartbeat felt like it would explode out of her chest. Without turning around, she knew it belonged to her brother, Alejandro. She didn't dare look into Alberto's eyes as she didn't know quite how to play this out. Of course she'd realized it was a strong possibility she'd run across someone she knew, including her brother, when they'd said yes to coming to California. Her luck it was Alejandro—the one person she didn't want to happen upon. Fate had not saved her after all.

Ignoring Alberto she scanned over his shoulders looking for a way out. Could she run away and escape? Not likely. It was too crowded. Either one or both of them would catch up to her and demand an explanation. The two men would eventually meet if she planned to keep seeing Alberto, and for now she did. After all they'd been through, she'd fallen for him—he was a drug and she wasn't ready to kick the habit.

"Bella?" Alejandro said again. He was closer now—right over her shoulder, maybe four feet away. Fine, fine, fine!

Now might as well be as good time as any to get this introduction over with.

Arabella sighed and slowed her breathing to calm her nerves. She turned around to face the music. "What are you doing here Alejandro?" she said in shaky voice. So much for the calm breathing.

"The more important question is what are you doing here? And who is this you're with?"

She felt Alberto's hand move to grip her waist. He'd gone from gently having his hand on her back as they'd walked through the festival crowds to definitely staking his claim to her. He had no idea Alejandro was her brother. She could rectify at least that.

"Alberto Gutiérrez, this is my brother Alejandro Gomez."

Alberto looked from Arabella to Alejandro. "Oh? You have a brother?"

"Yes, an annoying one!" She said piercing her eyes at her brother and willing him to behave. Alberto sounded a little off kilter. Perhaps he couldn't remember she'd mentioned a brother. Well maybe she hadn't.

"Hi Alejandro. I'm Alberto and I work with your sister back in Spain." He extended his hand and Alejandro did not offer his.

"Alejandro don't be rude!" She hissed from clenched teeth.

"Ummhmm. It's nice to meet you," Alejandro said matter of factly, with disdain and impatience. He didn't extend his hand to Alberto. Instead she noticed the two of them sizing up the other.

She cleared her throat and both men then looked at her. "What is it with you males acting like I'm some toy to fight over?"

Alejandro ignored her comment, instead saying, "Arabella I want to speak to you. Alone!" She knew he was angry whenever he addressed her as Arabella. She sighed.

She turned slightly and looked into Alberto's eyes, putting her hand on his forearm. "Alberto please excuse me for a moment while I set my brother straight."

"Are you sure?"

She nodded her head in an affirmative response. She felt like her worst nightmare had come true. And she was fighting back tears, a clear sign she'd reached a state of anger as well.

"Okay. I won't be far away."

"She's my concern, not yours. She'll be safe with me," Alejandro said facing off to Alberto. Alberto stepped forward refusing to back down from the challenge.

Arabella hated when men got into their pissing contests with each other. Especially when she was the subject of their power plays. She was not some pawn in a game. She wanted to yell at Alejandro to stop trying to boss her around. She was not going to step between them in a fight.

"Enough gentlemen! Don't make me walk away from both of you," she said in a measured calm she didn't feel.

Alberto must have heard her warning and backed off saying, "Si, por favor Bella. I will leave you two to talk."

"Thank you!" She mouthed to Alberto, and then she watched him moved away.

Arabella turned her attention to her brother. "Why did you have to be so ungracious? Mom would be so disappointed!"

"You didn't answer my call today? I was worried. Now I see you here and with some guy. Why didn't you tell me you were here?"

They could keep this banter up for hours. Or she could be the adult even if he was the eldest. "I'm truly sorry I didn't answer your call. It slipped my mind to turn my phone back on. I was sent here last minute for the festival. We're working."

"Doesn't look like work to me! You're coming home immediately!"

"I am not!"

"He's making a fool of you in front of others."

"Stop! Let's not get too far along being judgmental. I need you to set your ego aside and listen. I am on a work trip. We were sent here for the weekend from New York. It is a very short trip and we leave at dawn tomorrow. Also, I will be honest with you because I am grown and have nothing to hide. I am dating Alberto. I didn't plan it considering we work together, and I like him."

"Well, I don't like him. The way he looks at you is possessive. You need to end this and come home." True to her brother's take control attitude, he made demands and thought she'd concede this time yet again. While she'd heard Alejandro's edict, she refused to act like a child asking for permission to live her life.

She stared her brother in the eye and said in a calm voice that surprised even her, "you don't have to like him. He works with me. He's smart and we have much in common. I will keep seeing him as long as we both want." Technically, Alberto worked for her. Telling Alejandro that would only fuel the fire. "And for the record Alejandro, I am not coming back home!"

"He's using you for a good time. Like a Don Juan. And when he's done with you, he'll throw you away and be onto his next victim."

"He's not like that. And even if he were, no one has the power to use me. Yes, we are having an affair and I'm not wanting anything more than that right now."

"That's ridiculous. You are too precious for that kind of superficial relationship."

"I love you too my dear brother. I've got this."

"No you don't! You have no idea how men think. If you're offering, we'll take. If you don't demand a commitment, then he sure won't."

"Is that how you are Alejandro?" She watched her brother run his hand through his hair.

"Look this isn't about me. You're being stubborn and obstinate!"

"No brother, I'm finally living my life on my terms!"

"I don't want to argue in public with you Bella! I can see your mind is settled. I'll let this be for now."

"I love you even when you frustrate me."

"May I have a hug?"

"Yes my dear brother you may have a hug. I missed you!"

She threw her arms around her big brother and held on for dear life. They hugged for a long time. At some point he whispered to her, "I love ya to the moon and back."

"Love ya back and to the moon," she responded.

When they separated she looked at her brother—her hero. "Be happy for me. I'm doing well."

"I will, for now."

"Thank you Big Brother!"

"You're welcome Lil Sis! Enjoy the rest of the festival."

"Do you want to walk around with us for a while?" She hoped he wouldn't stay but her good manners made her ask.

"No I'm about to leave. I have dinner plans." She knew she'd just dodged a bullet.

"Oh? With who?"

"No one important. Be safe back to Spain"

"Hmph who's being evasive now?"

"Not I Sis! I'll leave that honor to you."

"Yeah okay! Bye for now!"

"Bye! And Bella, make sure you answer my call next Sunday."

She laughed, "I wouldn't dare miss it, I promise."

He kissed her gently on the cheek, turned and walked back into the crowd. She followed him with her eyes until she could see him no more. One little tear escaped her eyelid. She really did miss her brother and being in his space.

"You okay Bella?" She heard Alberto say as he came to stand behind her.

"Yeah sort of," she said turning to face him. "Seeing Alejandro made me miss being home."

"I understand." That was all he said. He put his arms around her and she was again comforted in knowing Alberto was here to help her pick up the pieces.

"Thank you." She was grateful for Alberto and his understanding.

Chapter 22

"She wanted something else, something different, something more. Passion and romance, perhaps, or maybe quiet conversations in candlelit rooms, or perhaps something as simple as not being second."
~ Nicholas Sparks, The Notebook (The Notebook, #1)

She heard a knock on her office door. "Come in." On the other side of the door was her friend, Lacey.

"Hi Arabella. I came to check on you."

"I'm doing really well."

"I also wanted to come by and tell you how much I appreciate our new friendship."

"I very much appreciate yours as well. I never realized how hard it would be to move to a new place without having family or friends there."

"You have a lot of heart, passion, and love to give. We are very lucky to have you here. You are like family."

Arabella sighed wistfully. "I just want to create a family of my own someday."

"Well did you tell Alberto that?"

"Tell who?" Arabella was suddenly wary as to where Lacey was going with this conversation.

"Alberto, of course!"

"Why would I tell him? You don't think there's something going on between Alberto and me, do you?"

Lacey laughed out loud. "Arabella, come now, it is obvious you and Alberto are involved."

Not having the energy to deny she had hopelessly fallen for him, she said "are we that obvious? I hope not!"

"In the last few weeks since the ball, yes. We've noticed that you two share a secret connection. No one was sure, and we had our suspicions. Alberto's eyes follow you every time you move."

"Oh, this is a disaster!"

"Not really. We are happy that stubborn man has met his match. He can be unbearable at times, they say. In your presence, it is comical to watch him capitulate to you."

"I don't know about that. He is stubborn, and can also be very charming at times."

"I bet. All the Gutiérrez men have that charm. Trust me. When Juan Carlos tells me no, he really means yes. He sometimes makes me work hard for a yes, and he always gives me my way in the end. Anyway, as I said before, perhaps Alberto wants a family too. You should tell him what you want. See what he says; he might surprise you!"

"No, there's really no point in telling him."

"Maybe he wants the same thing?"

"I doubt that. He wants to explore my "assets," my curves, and my desire to please him. He doesn't want me running his labs nor does he see me as part of his future."

"I don't know about that Arabella. I've seen how he looks at you for myself. I've seen how angry he gets when another man notices you."

"You are being too kind Lacey."

"I am not. Trust me. I watch people and not much gets past me."

"Why are you telling me all this?"

"I think all those red curls are too tightly warping your common sense. It's obvious to all of us that Alberto is in love with you."

"What? No way, not possible. He doesn't love me. Wait!" She paused. "What do you mean, all of us?"

"The entire family. We had a discussion after dinner last night."

Turning red faced, Arabella sank down in her chair. Oh now there's more to deal with! "We, who?"

Lacey paused. "Let's see. It was Juan Carlos, Olivia, Javier, Mama, Papa and me of course."

Arabella lifted her glasses from her eyes and set them amidst the mass of pinned-up curls atop her head. She rubbed her eyes as if weary from the revelation that just spilled from Lacey's mouth. "How did I become dinner conversation, Lacey? Please enlighten me?"

"Ummm, well, Papa asked how the transition is going and how well you are fitting in."

"Go on."

"My husband chuckled, looked over to Alberto and said, 'everything is going great, except when Alberto is being an ass!'"

"He said that?"

"Si. And Alberto cut him a dirty look."

"And?"

"Mama then said, 'Arabella, she's a nice woman, and very smart. I like her.' Javier, then laughed and said, 'so does Alberto!'"

"This just gets worse with every word! What did Alberto say?" Arabella was afraid of the answer.

"Alberto grunted, and cut his eyes into Javier. Then he said, 'I don't like that she took my job!' Then Juan Carlos said, 'get over it.' Alberto elbowed his brother, and Papa said, 'quit it,' to both of them."

That made Arabella laugh. "They still act like little children!"

"Oh yes! The fun part was then Mama spoke up saying, 'Well, I think Arabella's perfectly suited for you Alberto. Don't let her escape while you are busy being proud, arrogant, and stubborn!'"

"Oh my," Arabella said.

Lacey continued, "And then Alberto threw his napkin on the table and said in an angry voice, 'I wish everyone would mind their own damn business!' He got up and stormed off."

For a quick moment, Arabella's thoughts flashed back to Alberto's unannounced visit on her doorstep last night. He must have come from dinner to her. They didn't spend much time talking. Instead they opted for being consumed by their hot passion and making love.

"Are you listening, Arabella. You did ask for details."

Hearing Lacey, Arabella came back to present moment. "Oh right, go on!"

"Well when Alberto had stormed off, Papa asked why Juan Carlos and Javier were teasing their brother. Juan Carlos said, 'fair turnabout Papa. Alberto has been mercilessly talking crap to us.'"

"Then what happened?"

"Papa went on to say, 'it's early in their relationship, and the situation is complicated. Back off.' Mama squashed the discussion by pronouncing 'Alberto's already in love with her. They will get together and give me more grandbabies. I just want more babies,' she looked from each of us couples."

"Grandbabies? You and Juan Carlos recently married. Are you all trying to make babies?"

"Juan Carlos and I are not! At least not yet."

"That seems reasonable. So what happened next?" Arabella really wanted this conversation to end.

"Yes, Javier responded saying, 'In due time Mama. Don't rush us along,' and he winked over at Olivia and squeezed her hand on the table. Then he said he wants to spend a little time having it be just the two of them."

"Oh wow, that was awkward!"

"Not as much as it was when Javier went on to say 'I promise we are getting lots of practice on how to make babies.' Olivia, outright embarrassed, turned rosy red and lowered her head. Papa told Javier to stop embarrassing Olivia—neither of your wives are used to the antics of you boys!'"

"Yes, these brothers are definitely into mischief!"

"Agreed. Javier made it up to Olivia looking petulant and kissing her hand, and then made another pronouncement—'one thing I can promise is when we are ready, we want lots of babies.' Olivia smiled up at him and shook her head in agreement. Then Mama said, 'good as I am not going to live forever. If not for Marcelo, I would have no babies to spoil!'"

"Marcelo has taken a little bit of the pressure off the rest of you?"

"Yes, and while we all chuckled a little uneasily, Papa laughed heartily and said 'at the rate our sons are falling in the honey pot of love, Mama, we will have babies for many years to come.' Then Mama looked from Javier to

Juan Carlos, and said, 'your father better be right. If not, there will be hell to pay!'"

"What did you say to that?"

"Nothing. Thankfully, Juan Carlos said, 'I thought this conversation was about Alberto, not us. We've done great in picking our ladies. Why not focus on Alberto.'"

Back to Alberto again…the nightmare continues. "Hopefully, that ended the conversation?"

"Not quite! Mama wagged her finger and said, 'mark my words. I have no doubt, soon Arabella will be my daughter too. Alberto has already shown his hand by storming off tonight. He just can't see it yet. Too much of his papa in him. Enough already, it's time for me to retire.' She held out her hand to her husband, and said 'Come Papa! Let's leave the young people to their dessert, and we can go create our own.' Papa said, 'Si Mama, your wish is my command.' Papa jumped up to help Mama from her chair, and off they went."

"Wow, I am mortified!"

"Yes, everyone at the table was speechless, and also thankful that conversation ended."

Arabella shook her head. "Small favors that Alberto didn't stay."

"Arabella, I thought I'd warn you to run unless you really are interested in making this thing with Alberto permanent. If you want more, tell him; give him a future to live into—one that's not totally consumed with olive oil production. You might as well have some say right now. Because trust me, there is nowhere to hide from that matchmaking couple, Mama and Papa. When they set their minds, watch out!"

"I see that. Well you've given me a lot to consider. Thank you."

"Selfishly I want this thing with you and Alberto to work out so we'll be sisters in real life. However, the choice is yours. I have to go now. I promised Juan Carlos I would have lunch with him."

"Thanks again Lacey." The two women hugged. After Lacey left, Arabella thought about what she'd said. A family? With Alberto? I wonder what that might be like...

Chapter 23

"I love the way you lit candles, with the insistence that I never look, just so I can open my eyes and find the light in the darkness." ~ R. YS Perez, I Hope You Fall in Love: Poetry Collection

Arabella was at her desk and had to admit she was currently not in the best mood. She'd been shuffling through reports that she didn't understand for the last two hours. If she was being honest, it wasn't the reports, or the language barrier. Alejandro had just text to say 'Happy Thanksgiving - I miss you Lil Sis.' She'd looked from the phone to her desk calendar. November 22nd. Wow, she'd forgotten today was the fourth Thursday in November, an American holiday. The calendar on her desk was in Spanish so it didn't pick up American dates of importance.

What would she be doing if she was back home? That was a no-brainer. Henderson Winery always had a big celebration dinner at 4:00 pm in the afternoon that carried on into the wee hours of the morning as no one had to work the following day. Since her parents' death, she and Alejandro had volunteered annually in the early morning with Meals on Wheels in San Francisco where they'd delivered turkey dinners to those in need. Then they'd return back to the vineyard, have dinner and party with the big family of workers—people they called friends.

She heard the phone buzz again, and looked back to the screen. "You there, Sis?"

She picked up the phone. Fine! How should I reply? Yeah, I'm here? No, I'm ignoring you? She opted instead for "Yep! Thanks and Happy Thanksgiving Alejandro! I miss you back!"

"Thanks Sis!"

She guessed he was not going to let her get away with a simple hi and bye. "You're welcome! Where are you?"

"I'm on the way back from volunteering."

"Oh, you went without me?" Arabella didn't know why she'd not given any thought to the holiday, nor why she was agitated that he was continuing on with their tradition without her. What did it matter? Her brother was reaching out. She could be grateful she had such a thoughtful brother. In reality, she was beyond grateful he cared for her, even when he was being bossy!

"Yeah, I figured it would make me not miss you so much. It didn't work."

She didn't want to address how much she missed him or being home. Change the subject. "Okay. If you're driving, why are you texting versus calling?"

"I didn't want to bother you. Maybe I thought you might be sleeping. Are you?"

"You are my brother, never a bother. Plus, it's only 10:00 pm here; it's too early for sleep. I haven't even had dinner and I'm still at the office."

She saw the smile emoji he text back. And then the next line, that said "Figures! You work too much!"

She sent a laughing with tears emoji face back to him and the message, "Yeah okay. The only reason you are not at work is it's a national holiday."

"Touché Sis!"

"Stop texting and focus on driving. Have fun eating enough turkey for both of us!"

"I promise to eat more than enough! I love you to the moon and back!"

The tear she'd been fighting to ignore escaped her eye. She wiped it away and typed, "Be safe! I love ya back and to the moon!"

"Talk Sunday!"

"Deal! Now stop texting me! Focus on driving!" She ended the exchange, still moody and now present to how alone she was in the office. She ran her thumb back over the conversation with Alejandro. How could she forget Thanksgiving? Had she already assimilated to life in Spain so much so that she'd lost sense of her favorite holiday?

She put the phone down on the desk, took off her glasses and rubbed her eyes. It was getting late in the evening and she was tired. Today had been full of meetings and the never ending stack of paperwork sat staring at her from the corner of the desk. Evie, Alberto's assistant, had brought the reports to her office at 7:00 pm. Hmph, there is always more work to do!

Arabella considered her somber mood. Now was a stopping point where she might pack it up for the night and go home. The rest of the paperwork could wait until tomorrow morning. Deciding that was the best move, she began throwing papers into her leather sack and heard a knock on her office door. Who could that be? "Come in!"

"Hi Bella Bella!" Alberto said as he entered her office to stop just inside the doorway. His frame still took up most of the space. He was smiling at her.

She smiled back. "Hey funny one! What are you doing here?" She paused. "And why are you dressed in a suit? Wait! Did we have plans I forgot about? Am I late to meet you?" She paused again, sure they'd made no plans for tonight. "Or are you going out with someone else?" She tilted her head to await his reply. And she secretly said to herself, 'you better not be going out with someone else and stopping at my office first! I will kill you.' She wasn't really the jealous type. Yet she couldn't fathom why she had feelings of rage. Maybe it was because they'd been seeing each other constantly since the ball, with the exception of avoiding one other at Javier and Olivia's wedding ceremony. Oh wait, maybe she was easily angered because she didn't sleep around. One man at a time—it was all or nothing. Usually, it progressed to nothing if she got any clue another women existed.

"Now who's being the funny one," she heard him say.

She had gone off on her own tangent. What if he was only pretending to like her? What if there were a multitude of women he was seeing at the same time? They'd never had a conversation about being 'exclusive.' Did people even do that anymore?

"Stop that thinking Bella! I know where your mind just went. Let me be clear. I only have eyes for you!" He was still smiling yet the serious intent in his look burned her from across the room.

She blushed. Would she ever stop turning red with his compliments? "Okay! So why the suit?"

"Isn't this your American holiday called Thanksgiving?"

"Yea. And?"

"Well I thought maybe we could celebrate it together."

"How might we do that? It is not a Spanish holiday."

"Come," He said as he held out a hand and gently bowed his head. "I have a surprise for you!"

She didn't move. Instead she sighed. "Alberto, I don't like surprises! Where would we be going?"

"Bella, just trust me!"

"Okay, fine," she huffed out. "I was just getting ready to leave for the night anyway."

"That's good to hear. Then I don't have to kidnap you."

"Haha very funny!"

"I'm serious. I would if I needed to."

She picked up her purse and leather bag and put the straps of both on her shoulder. She slowly walked across the room to stand in front of him. What was his surprise? She had a feeling he wasn't going to fill her in on the details. She could try to find out more. "What about my car? Do I leave it here or follow you?"

"Always the detailed one. Follow me back to your place and then you can get into my vehicle."

"But, I'm not dressed to go out," she said as she looked down at her long black, pencil skirt, pale green blouse, and low-heeled, black shoes."

"What you have on is perfect."

"But, I don't look as good as..." He pulled her into his arms and kissed her mid-sentence. When he ended the kiss, all semblance of whatever was her last thought had disappeared. Breathless she uttered, "I'm ready to go now!"

"Awesome, let's go!" And off they went.

When they arrived at her cottage, Alberto suggested she get a sweater for the night air. She stepped inside the house, retrieved a sweater, locked up and slid into the passenger seat of his work car—a Mercedes GLS SUV. He'd turned on the radio to a soft music channel. She took the opportunity to ask another question about this surprise: "Want to fill me in now on where we're headed?"

"No." That was all he said. He's determined to keep mum about their destination. She didn't ask again. Instead she used the quiet time to decompress from her day. It was a nice, peaceful drive. Well it wasn't exactly peaceful to her. She was still chastising herself for forgetting Thanksgiving—to which even Alberto remembered! She was worried about this 'surprise' too. She was not unhappy, more like unsettled.

They rode for about ten more minutes and he turned off the interstate onto a country road. She'd assumed they were going into the city of Jaén. This latest turn was not the way into the city, unless they were taking a very back road. And she highly doubted that to be the case. Turning in her seat to face him, at least as much as the seat belt would allow, she asked again, "Where are you taking me Alberto?"

He put his hand up to his lips. "Shhhh, we're almost there. You cannot control everything Bella. I promise you will like it." He smiled at her again.

She half-heartedly rolled her eyes. "Really? You better hope I like it! Or else there will be hell to pay." Clearly he could see she was annoyed. Was he purposefully trying to anger her with the whole control label? The word 'control' seemed a little harsh. She didn't consider herself a 'control freak.' She looked down and started to fidget with her hands as they sat in her lap. She did maintain control in most of her life. Maybe she lacked spontaneity. Maybe she wasn't posh and polished like the women he normally dated. Does he think there's something wrong with me? Is dating a work colleague a big mistake? What if this all blows up in my face? How then will we keep working together? She was not scoring well when it came to this man.

"Here we are! Look!" He pulled the vehicle to a stop and cut the engine. She lifted her head up to see him pointing out the front windshield, and her eyes followed. They were in front of what she supposed was a small, rustic farmhouse amongst a grove of olive trees. The trees closest to the structure on both sides were peppered with a million lights. It was pitch black everywhere else, including the farmhouse. Wow...tree branches twinkling with dainty sparks under a thousand stars of the sky. This is magical! She wondered where they were.

Before she could say anything, Alberto had left the car and come around to open her door. "Senorita, welcome to Thanksgiving, Spanish style!"

Arabella put her hand into his outstretched one and stepped out. She walked five steps ahead and heard the door close behind her. She slowly gazed at the mesmerizing scene and outlying area. There was an outline of mountain hills, no lights or other signs of life for miles around. There seemed to be an old barn a few feet away from the back of house; it sat on the hillside, and looked to be decorated with a harvest theme with bales of straw hay and pumpkin like squashes. From the side of the house, there was a simple stone path with low level and recessed lights that she'd not originally seen from the SUV.

Arabella placed her hand over her lips. What words would convey the beauty of this scene? She slowly turned back to face the man who was responsible for it all. "My goodness. What have you done Alberto? This is spectacular! When did you have time to do all this? How..."

He pulled her into his arms and kissed her mid-sentence. Again he'd silenced her with his kiss! Again wow, she thought as he lifted his lips from hers!

Looking down at her, he said "I will answer one question, querida. Choose wisely."

No pressure there, huh? There was only one thing she wanted to fiercely know. "Why'd you do all this for me Alberto?"

"I figured you might be homesick."

He knew! She paused. "Thanksgiving is my favorite holiday. I'd forgotten all about it until I got a reminder just before you popped up at my office door."

"Querida, you are a world away from your traditions and culture. It can't be easy. If I could've, I would've sent you home for Thanksgiving. I knew you wouldn't have gone. So I created the next best thing."

She remained silent. She too knew she would not have gone home. Instead she could just picture she'd have been stubborn and obsessed with proving she wasn't homesick.

"Do you like it?" His words cut into her thoughts.

"Yes very much! Thank you! This is an amazing fairy tale scene." The night air was chilly, but Arabella was warm and toasty inside. No one had ever gone through so much trouble for her. Just then she heard music playing in the not too far off distance. It sounded like from a violin or some type of stringed instrument. "And that music that just started, where is it coming from?"

"The cello," he said in a matter of fact manner.

"What cello?"

"Come, I will show you" he said, placing his hand into hers and gently pulling her along towards the barn.

Once there, he opened the door for her to walk in ahead of him. There were string lights hanging from the wood beams and what looked to be a hundred small artificial candles sitting on bales of hay at various levels scattered around the room and across the wood floors. The candlelight twinkled every few seconds, giving one a surreal experience. It was a traditional barn, turned into pure romance any woman would appreciate.

As Arabella walked in the space, the music got louder, yet it still held soft, classic tones. She turned her head in the direction of its sound. There just off to right of the entrance sat a woman soloist playing the cello. She was dressed in a deep, rich brown colored gown that was a perfect complement to the instrument she held. Her hair delicately framed her face with lose tendrils; her cat-like eyes shining with life for the music she played. She nodded a smile as they entered and never missed a beat. Arabella of course smiled back. She'd already begun to feel the passion of the maestro as her bow and fingers glided across the strings.

Alberto put his arms around Arabella's waist, pulled her back against him and whispered in her ear, "No, I don't know her so don't get jealous. Evie procured her services, and helped me create tonight especially for you. I came up with most of the ideas, and Evie hired the people. This place, it is an old farmhouse on the back end of our property. Newer homes were built for our caretakers and this one was left behind."

As he talked, she let her head rest back against his chest, finding comfort in his strong arms. "Evie! That little rat. She never let on about any of this. She even dropped off some reports this evening before going home."

"That's one of her many talents—discretion."

"She's beautiful, our cellist," Arabella said as she stared at the woman. "And the music she plays, oh so enticing."

"I hadn't noticed. And I don't care about her. I care about you. Let's go sit down."

It wasn't a request, it was a demand. He let his arms fall from around her and led the way to the center of the space—a table formally set for two. The chairs were covered with a simple slipcover that matched the table's crisp white linens. As Alberto held out a chair for her and she sat, she noticed the rest on the decor—thick pillar candles surrounded by hurricane glass, crystal glassware, china plates and silverware. The lit candles gave off a luminescent, soft glow that made the barn look like the ideal place to have dinner. There was also a simple garnish of leaves decorated with lemons—an aroma that permeated the air. She suspected the leaves hailed from the olive trees outside. A nice touch! Elegant and simplistic—traits Arabella admired even in the fanciest of settings. Her parents had loved their simple life, set amidst opulence and wealth. They'd raised her and Alejandro to work hard and appreciate life's simplicities. Perhaps Alberto was like that too. She never really thought about settling down for a simple life. He made her think of such things. He made her want in new ways. When she lifted her eyes to look at the man who'd seated himself across the table from her, his eyes were watching her. "What?" she asked.

"You look absolutely breathtaking in the candlelight. I never imagined such beauty would be in my life, in my presence."

She immediately blushed. What do I do with that? He's so charming. Damn him for making me have to respond! "Thank you. I think you are just trying to get me in a good mood!"

"Is it working?" He looked almost unsure of himself. She wasn't used to that.

"A little," she said as she smiled.

He smiled back.

"I do mean it. Thank you for doing all of this. I am not used to such gestures. As you mentioned in the car," she paused. And then cleared her throat. "I do try to control my behavior for the most part. So I don't usually find myself in these types of situations. "

"I love to watch you lose control in my arms, querida. When we make love, you are unbounded, a free spirit. We are a lot alike, you and I. Always buried in our work. There are moments in time when I just want to relax and forget everything else. I am like that when I am with you."

Wow, he'd summed up her feelings. "I feel the same."

"I am glad I could spoil you for a few moments. Treat you to a simple, elegant evening without much fuss. Just the two of us and no work or outside distractions."

"Well it seems to me you went through a lot of trouble to create tonight."

"Not at all. And even if I did, you are worth it. Now how about some wine?"

"Yes, wine would be lovely."

He reached over to the bucket on a stand near the table. He lifted and poured the already opened white wine from the bottle into her goblet. Then he poured some into his. Placing the bottle back in its cradle, he lifted his glass towards her. "Cheers to a wonderful evening."

She lifted her glass to gently clank his. "Cheers to that," she uttered back.

As if on cue, a waiter appeared from somewhere in the recesses of the building. Alberto said, "Dinner is served."

And dinner was served. First course was a squash soup, with petite croutons. Then a salad made with three kinds of roasted beets, candied pecans, and goat cheese. The main course was both pheasant and turkey, yams, stuffing and petite string beans. For dessert, lemon olive oil cake, apple pie and vanilla ice cream. The whole meal had been a blend of the old with the new. By the time coffee was served, Arabella truly felt like she'd been at a Thanksgiving feast back home. She was stuffed!

They'd made small talk throughout their meal. She genuinely enjoyed conversations with him. He was always willing to talk about any subject, share his views and allow for her contradictory ones. There were very few topics they both agreed on—everyone deserved a quality education, poverty in society should no longer exist in these current times, and Alberto's mom is an amazing cook! Still as unlikely as it might sound, they were not opposites. There was a compatibility she couldn't put into words.

"Will you dance with me?" His request invading her thoughts.

"I'm pretty full. I don't know if I can move."

"Just one dance, a slow one."

How could she deny him anything? "I suppose one dance will be fine."

He appeared at her side and pulled back her chair. She arose on her feet, placed her napkin on the table, and steadied herself to walk. Then he placed his hand at the small of her back and moved her a few feet to an empty space. She really was stuffed, yet she was excited to be close to him, be held by him. He'd made this evening magical for her. She was so grateful.

Alberto put his arms around her. And she placed her right arm on his shoulder, her left on his arm. He began to move them very slowly as was his promise. She leaned her head on his chest. A perfect night with the perfect man. He is perfect. I love him. What? She stopped dancing.

"Bella, are you okay? Are you dizzy? Should we sit?"

She didn't realize he'd noticed her stop for the moment. She lifted her head to look up at him. "Ummm no, I'm good. Almost tripped over my own feet. Please continue."

"Okay." They resumed their previous positions. He again moved them slowly and she followed. After a couple of calming breaths she settled down. She accepted the mere fact that she'd fallen in love with him. How could she not? He'd been an all-around great guy. Well maybe not in the beginning. But certainly before they'd fallen into bed the night of the ball. He listens to her, lets her be herself and is not afraid to challenge her. He considers her needs and what it's like for her to be away from home.

As he ended the dance, she breathed a sigh of contentment and lifted her head. She looked up into his eyes as he looked down searching hers. Oh gosh...she was in trouble now. She was lost in their depth. Say something. "Alberto, you are an amazing man. Thank you again for doing all of this for me."

"The pleasure is mine querida." He moved a piece of hair away from her left eye. "I want to tell you something."

"Oh, that I am a lousy dancer when stuffed?" She smiled.

"No. I want to tell you...I love you Bella. I'm in love with everything about you!" He smiled a quirky kind of smile, almost like a schoolboy who was shy and unpracticed around girls.

Oh wow! He loves me? He loves you! You love me?

"Say something Bella?"

She smiled, gently reached her right hand up to his cheek and caressed his razor stubbled skin. "That's good news Alberto, because I'm in love with you too!"

"Really?" He said as he stepped back, still not letting her go. "Are you sure?"

"Yes, really you incorrigible man!"

He leaned over and lowered his head to capture her lips in the most alluring and seductive kiss ever. And she'd experienced quite a few with him over the course of their short relationship. She had a brief thought what might the cellist think? Who cares? Kiss him back like no one's watching. She was on fire for this man and wouldn't mind a roll in the hay. Really, like here in this barn...right now over on the hay stack!

All too soon Alberto stopped kissing her. No don't stop was her first cohesive thought. Why, why, why do you keep stopping was the next? They were both breathing heavily now. He broke the silence first.

"As you might be able to tell, I am happy with you loving me too. I could take you right here. But now is not the time nor the place. I best get you home for the night."

She was disappointed he wasn't going to immediately take her here acting on their passion. And she understood. She shook her head yes in agreement. He then took her hand and led her back out into the magical night. She looked over her shoulder one more time to always remember this place where they'd said 'I love you' to one another for the very first time. It was truly special.

The trip back to her place was quiet. She curled up in her seat facing him, and he held her hand intertwined across the console. All too soon, he was pulling up to her doorstep. He got out of the driver's seat and came around to open the door for her as always. She stepped down and walked into his arms. "Come spend the night with me Alberto."

He hugged her back. "Not tonight, my Bella."

"What do you mean not tonight?" she said as she moved herself back to look at him.

He let his hands fall from her and down to his side. He ran his hand through his hair. She waited. "I'm not going to come in tonight."

"Wait. Are you refusing to stay with me, to make love to me?"

"Yes, for once, I am. It is not easy to do. Trust me."

She stared at him in dismay. "Then why do it?"

"I don't want you to think I said 'I love you' as a one off. Or just to get you into bed!"

"You've already gotten me in bed. Numerous times, I might add."

"Not this time Bella. I am a gentleman. Tonight was about you, and celebrating your favorite tradition. It was to say thank you for sacrificing so much in coming here to help our company. Not a ruse to have my way with you."

She was confused and disheartened. Maybe Alberto's refusal hurt. The honorable thing wasn't always the easiest. She exhaled slowly. "Okay, I get it's not over for us. For one night, fine! How I wanted tonight to end has nothing to do with all the gifts you gave me this evening. I will not act like a spoiled child being denied another piece of candy. I respect your decision."

"Thanks for understanding my logic!"

"Well let's not get too carried away. I don't get it. And I know when you've made up your mind, it will be hell to pay tomorrow for everyone else if I leave you in a foul mood."

"Point made. May I have a kiss goodnight Bella Bella?" He smiled again knowing his silly nickname for her would alter the mood.

"Yes, a chaste one," she said with her most alluring look and held up her cheek for him.

He placed a simple kiss on her right cheek. "Goodnight my love. Sweet dreams! It's so not over for us. Not by a long shot."

She touched her fingers to the place his lips had just been. "Goodnight Love." And then she turned and walked into the house. Door closed, she leaned back against it on wobbly legs. She sighed. What a night! I love him and he loves me! I'm frustrated as hell too that he didn't come in and finish what he started. No sweet dreams for me tonight...

Chapter 24

"The secret of a happy marriage is finding the right person. You know they're right if you love to be with them all the time." ~ *Julia Child*

Sunday dinner at Casa Gutiérrez was just about over. Dessert was being served. Alberto had settled for a bowl of limon gelato. He wasn't in the mood for cake too—he really hadn't been hungry all evening. He just went through the motions so Mama wouldn't fuss. For most of the meal, he'd contemplated all that was on his mind. Conversations continued even as food plates had come and gone. Through it all, everyone in attendance seemed to be enjoying their time together.

Papa sat at the head of the table with Mama at his side. The order of seating was often rearranged to accommodate special guests. Tonight was one of the few rare times in recent days where Alberto was not in the seat next to his father. Sadly, the lucky one was their brother, Tomas Miguel or TM as they call him for short. He'd come home for the weekend or more likely he was summoned.

Alberto heard through the grapevine his 'playboy' brother had gotten himself into some international drama and photos were plastered all over the tabloids. Supposedly last weekend TM abruptly left a royal charity function to instead go party on a yacht in the French Rivera. It wouldn't have been a big deal if he'd not also taken with him the princess whose father was hosting the event. TM's behavior brought shame to the Gutiérrez family name and his parents couldn't ignore it this time. Alberto was sure Papa had quietly lectured TM most of dinner. Giving TM his way and excusing his behavior all these years was finally too much. Alberto didn't envy either TM or his parents. The time had come for their baby brother to grow up and be responsible. How that would happen, no one knew exactly. For now, TM would have to mind his manners and serve his penance.

Alberto looked around to check in on other conversations. Also in attendance tonight were Juan Carlos, Lacey, cousins Stefano, Eduardo, and Valentino. They were all invested in a debate with Lacey over types of chocolate and which country had the best. Their sister-in-law preferred Belgian chocolates over all others. Personally, Alberto was not a huge chocolate fan, but he enjoyed it on occasion. He suspected Lacey especially loved Belgian varieties because that's where she and Juan Carlos fell in love, in the Belgian town of Bruges. Juan Carlos agreed with his wife, which was not a surprise. Stefano was espousing the virtues of German chocolate; Eduardo claimed all the real chocolate aficionados already knew Swiss chocolate to be the very best; and Valentino who was in for a business meeting from Cape Town refused to choose. It was a lively night, and just what Mama loved—family time around a big table. Alberto hoped Mama would keep getting stronger from her surgery.

He loved being around his family with all their opinions and differing perspectives. And even with all that was going on, he needed their assistance to move forward in the 'right way.' He didn't quite know how to broach the subject of Bella with them. The family now knew that they were dating after he'd brought her to last week's dinner. Word spreads fast around here. He'd gone from angry tyrant to love sick puppy, and they seemed happy for him. He really didn't care per se. As long as his family thought his love interest was a good person, they'd shown in the past that the woman would be welcome. Not that he'd brought many women home. Maybe two over the course of twenty years. Mama was the key, and she was a huge Bella supporter. If not for Mama's dictate when Bella first came to the company, he might still be angry and at war.

Not anymore! Bella was meant for him. She was a beautiful woman with a good head on her shoulders. They'd forged a good working relationship in the office, and an even better one everywhere else. As a couple, they'd gotten to know each other a lot better away from Spain and the pressures of the family business.

While in New York, they'd attended conference sessions and were able to network, secure new distribution channels for export, and conduct impromptu meetings. In California, even though there was work to do, they'd had lots of fun adventures and were able to relax. Sightseeing was going great until they'd unexpectedly run into Bella's brother, Alejandro, at an olive oil festival. It could have ended his new relationship if not for Bella's determination and declaration she had every intention to return to Spain. He could still remember how she'd stood up to her brother. Alberto would have leveled Alejandro for insinuating that Alberto was only using Bella for a good time. She stepped between them in the midst of a testosterone battle, simply saying 'stop or you will both lose me.' That stopped them both dead in their tracks. No more hiding out and do right by my sister—that was the clear message Alejandro had conveyed. Alberto's message was stay out of our relationship.

Even if Alberto didn't particularly care for Bella's bossy brother, he'd been correct about how special and rare Bella is and she deserved everything—including being respected and publicly adored. Never should anyone whisper behind her back or wonder about her status—which was officially 'off the market and unavailable.' Even if Bella didn't want to deal with what other people thought about their relationship, Alberto was done keeping his feelings for her from the world. He was done watching other men vie for her attention and think they had any chance to be with her. They didn't. She belonged with him, and he loved her more than he'd ever loved another person, including his parents. No one would get in the way of that. In fact, Alberto was now determined to spend his life with Bella—for them to get married and have babies as Mama always talked about wanting for her sons. He was unsure what his family would say about wanting to marry Bella. He'd stormed off before from this very table over the subject of Bella. Would they help him make it special for Bella? Would they be happy for them? Would they welcome her to the family as his fiancé and with open arms? Hell, would she even accept his proposal?

Only Evie, had any idea how deep his feelings for Bella. He'd secretly started looking at wedding rings weeks ago and asked Evie for reputable jewelers. She'd masked her surprise well, made a couple of suggestions in town, and some in Granada too. He'd been searching for the perfect sapphire. Blue was Bella's favorite color. On numerous occasions, he'd noticed she wore blue accented jewelry or pieces accented with sapphires. He'd not yet picked out 'the ring,' but he would soon. And when he did, he'd do anything to get her to say yes. Including having his family openly bring her into the fold. How hard could it be?

He cleared his throat and spoke loud enough for everyone to hear. "I have some news."

Everyone stopped their individual chatter. All eyes now peering at him. It's now or never...

"Yes Son?" Papa granted him their collective attention.

"I am going to ask Bella to marry me, and I need the family's help!"

"You what?" Papa yelled, leaning over to get a good look at him three places away. His brothers and cousins snickered, and he smirked at them. He saw TM breathe a sigh of relief and slouch back in his chair as he was no longer the one in the hot seat. This was all so surreal. It was like they were little kids again avoiding getting into trouble.

He spoke slowly. "I want to surprise Arabella with a proposal of marriage here at Christmas dinner."

"Yes!" said Mama jumping up from her seat to go around Papa and the others to stand next to him. She placed her hand on his shoulder. "What a wonderful idea mi hijo!"

"Slow down Catherine," Papa said to his wife.

Mama was silent, but she didn't remove her hand of support from his shoulder. Alberto refused to look away from his father, even if he wanted nothing more than to hide behind his mother's apron like he was a child again. He was a man now, and had finally found the woman who completed him. He would wage any war necessary to marry her. Out of respect though he waited for his father to continue.

"Aren't you moving a little fast mi hijo?" Papa questioned in a quieter voice looking wary of Mama. People tread lightly when Mama stated her wishes.

Juan Carlos injected. "It is a little soon Alberto. She's not pregnant, is she?"

"How dare you ask that at my dinner table," Mama said chastising Juan Carlos.

More snickering from his cousins.

"Sorry Mama!" Juan Carlos said in a reverent tone.

It was time to take control. "Thanks Mama. I can appreciate all the questions. And the facts remain: you all brought Bella here to our company, gave her my job and then told me to be nice to her. I did what you asked. Now that we've fallen in love, you want to give me grief and say it's too soon. Well that's too bad. And it changes nothing."

"Papa, may I speak to you privately for a moment?" Mama was clearly agitated. When their parents were not on the same page, they'd discuss it privately and always come to consensus.

"Yes dear." Papa said almost sounding remorseful. He got up and led the way as they left the room. No one moved or said a word. They all lowered their heads to ponder what might happen.

Three minutes later, his parents returned to the room holding hands. They all watched as Papa held out Mama's chair so she could sit. Then he sat back in his place at the head of the table and reached out for Mama's hand. She placed hers into his. It really was bizarre to have parents still in love after forty years of marriage. Then Papa turned his focus to Alberto.

"Calmer heads prevail mi hijo. Mama talked some sense into me." He smiled over to his wife, and then back to his son. "This is your life Alberto. Not that you need it, but you have our blessing to marry Arabella. We'd be honored to have your proposal happen here during Christmas dinner. It will bring joy to my wife, and for that blessing, we all win!"

Alberto was speechless. Say something! What was appropriate to respond? And how could one go wrong with gratitude. "Thank you Papa! And Mama, I appreciate all you've already done to make Bella feel welcome."

"You're welcome hijo," Papa said. Mama just smiled and nodded her head. Now that it was settled, Alberto would follow up with Mama to arrange the details of his surprise. He just hoped Bella would show up and say yes. He'd know soon enough as Christmas was just a few weeks away. And he had one more loose end to tie up.

Chapter 25

"Science and technology revolutionize our lives, but memory, tradition and myth frame our response."
~ Arthur M. Schlesinger

"Hello."

"May I speak to Alejandro Gomez?"

"Speaking. Who is this?"

"Alberto Gutiérrez."

"Is Bella alright?"

"Yes, Bella is doing great!"

"Then what do you want?"

Alberto took a quick breath. He didn't have any sisters but he could sort of understand Alejandro's animosity and desire to protect Bella. Since their parents were no longer alive, it was the right thing to do to ask Alejandro for her hand in marriage. And he'd prepared for this call to test his patience.

"Did you hear me? What do you want?"

"Si, I heard you. I am calling to tell you that you were right. I was being selfish in not going public with our relationship. Bella wanted to keep it quiet and I complied until we returned from California. We've rectified that and now everyone here knows."

"Yeah Bella told me."

"Excellente. I wasn't sure she'd tell you after our rocky start. Anyway, your sister is an amazing woman and scientist. She is my heart and I love her. I want to marry Bella and I want your blessing to ask for her hand."

"You already know I'm not a fan of yours. I think you're an arrogant ass. And I am sure you think the same of me. Does Bella love you?"

"Si, she says she does."

"Man, this is impossible. I don't want Bella to be mad at me. She's brilliant. So if she loves you, then you must be an okay guy. Giving my blessing is not even personally about you. I'm not sure I want to give anyone permission to marry my sister. She means the world to me and I hate she's so far away. If she marries you, she'll never come home to stay."

"Look, I can understand you don't know me or my family. I love her with all that I am. I will surround her with family and provide for her, not that she needs anyone to do that. We are perfect mates and have so much in common. Plus, we're really happy together." Alberto heard the sigh on the other end of the call.

"While I don't like you, it's not my place to choose for Bella. She has to make up her own mind. If she wants to marry you, she will. I won't stand in her way."

"Thank you!"

"Don't thank me yet. It is Bella's choice."

"I have one more request. Will you come to Jaén? I want to propose to Bella at Christmas dinner with the family. It's a surprise. You being here will make it perfect."

"You're asking a lot." Alberto let the silence go on. "Fine, I'll think about it," Alejandro finally said.

"I really do want to get along with you. And I want you to meet my family too. We are six brothers who are close. Bella is already a part of our family regardless of the relationship she and I created. Mama took her under her wing from day one, let her stay in the estate's cottage, sent food, and kept Bella grounded even in a new place."

"I will let you know the week before Christmas." The phone clicked off.

Alberto thought that wasn't as bad as it could have been. Now all he needed to do was plan his surprise proposal and ensure Bella said yes.

******

Bella was daydreaming! About who else? Alberto. Since they'd had Thanksgiving together, they'd been seeing a lot more of each other. While she wasn't at all comfortable with being the subject of conversation at the Gutiérrez dinner table, she was starting to enjoy spending more time with Alberto. There was a knock on her office door and before she could say come in, Alberto walked through.

"I brought you something."

"Why?" Arabella picked up her pencil and started to chew the eraser on the end. She had a bad habit of mutilating any pencil when she was nervous.

"Because I care."

"Care about what?"

"You! I care about you."

She stopped chewing the pencil and narrowed her eyes. "Ummmhmm. Why else?"

"It's not what you think."

"What is it?"

"I will show you."

She slowly began to look at him from top to bottom. She hoped it was not more jewelry. She still hated when rich men bought females jewelry or sent them off shopping. It was so dismissive. She noticed Alberto was not moving from the spot he occupied. He looked amused by her perusal. She was not amused.

"Where is it?"

"Out there," he pointed to the outer office from whence he just came.

"I don't want it!" She hoped it was not a puppy or something she would have to send back.

He laughed. "You don't even know what it is!"

"And?" He smiled, clearly following her train of thought.

"And I don't need you buying me anything."

"I wanted to do something nice for you. Hold on." He walked out the door.

She was taken a back with his last pronouncement. He wanted to do something nice for me, she mouthed to herself? Men did not often ever want to do nice things for her.

She heard the rattle of bags as he reappeared. In his hands were two really big sacks of what looked like takeout food. "I brought us dinner."

Again Arabella was speechless. She was not sure what he had brought her, and food was the last she had expected. "You brought us dinner?"

"Si. I figured you would be starving since lunch was eight hours ago. I was on my way to pick up my favorite takeout, and I said why not get enough for two. I suspected you would still be working. Trust me, I understand the demands of your position. It never ends."

"Okay I do like that you thought of me. I'm starving for food."

"I guess I thought you might have some appreciation for me too."

"Oh I do and I will show you just how much after dinner!"

"Let's hurry up and eat!" She laughed a hearty laugh.

Chapter 26

"Everything is theoretically impossible, until it is done."
~ Robert A. Heinlein

It had been a long day and it wasn't even five o'clock. Alberto had skipped siesta and was pouring over the reports from the samples taken. Everything looked to be on track for a good harvest. The phone buzzed. Alberto picked it up. It was a text message from Alejandro. "Yes, I'll come for Christmas."

He opened the message to respond. "Thank you. Not just for Bella's sake, but for our future."

"Yeah, yeah. I'm still not a fan of yours."

"Give it time!"

"Maybe!"

"I will send the company jet for you."

"No thanks. I can arrange my own travel. I'll arrive Christmas Eve. "

"Will you come stay at our family home? My mother will insist!"

"Look I said I'd come for Bella, not to stay with your family."

"I know this is awkward considering our brief history. And I think for Bella's sake we need to become friends."

"You keep asking the impossible! I've never been friendly with anyone Bella's dated. I don't plan to start now!"

Alberto read the message and set the phone down. He ran his hand across his stubbly chin. How do I create peace with someone who is being impossible? How would my beloved Bella handle this? With kindness. What had she told him a thousand times...kill them with kindness? He respected Alejandro and was grateful he watched over his sister, especially after their parents died. He'd have been exactly the same if he'd any female siblings. An idea was forming. Alberto picked up the phone again and resumed typing. "Here's our opportunity then as I will be around longer than any other man she's ever dated or will date. I intend to marry your amazing sister. So to create peace in my home...for the rest of our lives, I'm going to be genuinely nice to you even if you refuse to be nice to me. And I'll leave it to Bella to deal with you..."

He waited for the response. When after a couple of minutes there was no answer, he set the phone down, spun around in his chair to look out the window, and steeped his fingers. Alberto knew his message was received loud and clear. He'd wait for the response. About ten minutes later, the phone buzzed. He turned back around.

The new message from Alejandro said, "as much as your existence annoys me, I almost like you. You are very shrewd and observant. And you know as well as I do, I will not disappoint Bella. Nor do I want her on my case."

He smiled to himself. Victory! Yes Alberto suspected his approach hit the right cord. "Great! I'll tell Mama so she can prepare a guest suite for you. I plan to pick you up from the airport, so please arrive before one in the afternoon. We both know it is hard to keep Bella in the dark about anything and the earlier you arrive, the more distracted she'll be with work."

"Wait, I have to ride with you from the airport?"

"Oh yes, I wouldn't miss out on bonding time with my soon to be brother-in-law. If we need to fight it out, then we have plenty of open fields."

"Haha, you'd lose."

"I would if it means I get to win Bella as my wife!"

"Touché, Alberto."

"See you soon Alejandro!"

"I'll send my itinerary when I have the exact arrival time."

"Looking forward to it." Alberto was pretty pleased with himself. He set the phone down on the desk. Now he could refocus on work. Just a couple weeks and he'd have his future set!

Chapter 27

"Here's an olive branch. Let's see what you do with it."
~ Todd Jones

Alberto drove his pickup truck to the airport. While he'd previously made up his mind to be nice to Bella's brother, he wasn't trying to put on any pretenses. Yes he and his family had substantial assets, were well respected and contributed to their community. But he didn't need to impress Alejandro. Both families had instilled in their children the foundation of education and a work ethic. Alejandro's focus is on Alberto's character and determining if he was a good match for Bella. And he was!

He pulled in and parked on the waiting lot. Based on the flight itinerary Alejandro sent, there were about fifteen minutes left before his scheduled arrival. Alberto passed the time by practicing meditation. Two calming breaths. Focus! Let all your thoughts go. Breathe. Repeat. He'd just about calmed his mind when the phone buzzed. He picked it up. The message read, "I've landed."

He typed back, "Welcome to Spain. I'll be out front standing next to a black pickup truck."

"Okay."

About ten minutes later Alberto watched as his beloved's brother emerged into the cold morning sunshine. He was dressed in jeans, flannel shirt, a Patagonia jacket, and was carrying a leather garment bag. They had a lot in common—they wore similar styles of dress, both worked in agriculture, and were very protective of those they love. If Bella didn't happen to be the love of his life and also Alejandro's sister, he suspected they'd have been great friends. Perhaps with time they would forge that kind of bond. Alejandro turned slightly and Alberto raised his hand to identify himself. He turned and strolled over.

When Alejandro had reached the vehicle, Alberto put out his hand to greet him. "Welcome to my home Alejandro."

Brooding and looking rough around the edges, Alejandro replied, "Yeah thanks." He didn't reach out to shake Alberto's offered hand so Alberto retracted it.

"Ready to go? We have an hour's drive to Jaén proper."

"Yeah, I'm exhausted. It's been endless hours of flying."

"Well I'll take you to the palazzo where my parents live. There you'll be free to rest."

"Great. Let's go!"

The time for small talk was over. So Alberto walked around to the driver's side and climbed in. Alejandro put his bag in the truck's backseat and got in too. Once they'd reached the interstate, Alberto decided it was time to broker a new peace.

"Look Alejandro. I'm grateful you came. What's it going to take for us to get along?"

"Time."

"Okay, I'll agree to give it some time. Might we also agree to one more condition?"

"What's that?"

"Let's agree to never argue or fight in front of Bella. She doesn't need to have to choose sides. That would be cruel to her."

"You really do love my sister!" It was a statement not a question.

"Yes I do! And I'll do anything to protect her from being upset."

There was more quiet silence. "I'll agree to that condition."

"Thank you!"

"Yeah, yeah. It's all for Bella. Now can we stop talking for the rest of the ride?"

Alberto nodded and said no more.

******

Alberto opened the door of Casa Gutiérrez to usher Alejandro through and into the formal living room. There he saw his parents lounging on the couch. Mama was reading a book with her feet on Papa's lap as he read the paper. Even with every luxury and amenity, his parents were such a normal couple. No one would ever know there was a billion dollar corporate conglomerate being run within their family.

"Papa, Mama, I want to introduce you to Alejandro Gomez, Arabella's brother. "

"Hello mi hijo!" Papa said. Mama moved her feet, Papa folded the paper and got up.

"Mr. and Mrs. Gutiérrez, it is a pleasure to meet you. Please don't get up on my account."

"Nonsense young man. We are very happy you've arrived." Papa said in English. Mama was behind Papa and by that time they made it across the room, they were in even step. Standing in front of Alberto and Alejandro, Papa reached out and shook Alejandro's hand.

Mama spoke up, "It's nice to meet you Mr. Gomez. I'm a hugger so I hope you don't mind a hug over a handshake." She held open her arms for a quick hug. Alejandro awkwardly leaned in to hug her and Alberto suppressed a smirk. Perhaps his parents were a little too forward and frank. Making Alejandro uncomfortable was admittedly easy to watch.

"Thank you Mrs. Gutiérrez! Please call me Alejandro."

"Very well! And we insist you call us Catherine and Antonio."

"Yes ma'am!" Alberto watched his mom frown. Alejandro must have noticed too. "Yes, I will call you Catherine."

"Lovely! Really it is okay to call me anything other than 'ma'am.' That title makes me feel old!"

"I'll try to remember that."

"Let's sit down for a few minutes? I'll ring for some tea."

"Of course." Alejandro had simply agreed to sit and chat. Little did he know his mother had mastery in discovering information as her victim became prey with no escape! Alberto would excuse himself as soon as possible to return to work—a move to get the focus off himself.

Mama and Papa returned back to the couch. Alberto and Alejandro settled for sitting on an identical set of wingback chairs across from his parents.

"Your kindness toward my sister has been a comfort to me since I live so far away in California."

Papa replied. "It is Arabella to whom we owe much. We are grateful she came to make our company stronger. "

Mama chimed in, "Yes and she has made us all even happier by taming our son, Alberto."

"Mama, really?" Alberto said half-jokingly.

"Yes really! Arabella is the blessing to our lives. Not only has she brought innovative ideas, she's patiently worked with the team to implement them. She's loved us, our culture and our family. We are all the better for her. Including you, our son!"

"I won't deny how much I love Bella. We all clearly cherish her too. Anyway, I would love to stay for tea and snacks. However, I need to return to the office."

"You and Bella are such workaholics. Very well. We'll watch over Alejandro."

"Thanks Mama." He went over to kiss his mother. They exchanged kisses on both cheeks, and she ruffled his hair as she often did when they said goodbye. "Papa, I'll call later if I can get away to come help you with set up for tomorrow."

"Thanks mi hijo!"

Finally Alberto turned to his guest. "Alejandro, I leave you in my parents' capable hands. I will be back later. If you need anything, you have my number."

"Okay." That was all he said.

On the way to the door, he turned back to say. "Remember everyone, mum's the word that Alejandro's is here in residence until tomorrow's Christmas dinner surprise."

"We know. We'll keep your secret!" Papa said.

As Alberto ran down the front steps to his pickup truck, he assessed his last couple of hours. Overall he thought the ride from the airport went extremely well. The introduction to his parents was also well received. Things were looking up! He still had a few hours to endure Alejandro's presence before he proposed to Bella. Verbal arguments he could handle; he just hoped they wouldn't get into any physical skirmishes in the meantime as those might be harder to hide from Bella.

Chapter 28

"And then my soul saw you and it kind of went, 'Oh, there you are. I've been looking for you.'"
~ Iain Thomas, I Wrote This For You

"Merry Christmas Bella Bella! Breakfast is served!"

Arabella lifted her head and squinted her eyes to see Alberto laying a tray on her bed. When had he escaped the bed? She was face down on her stomach and tangled in the bedsheet. She probably looked a mess. She'd been in a deep sleep, and was now waking up to his sinfully delicious voice—a sound she never got tired of hearing. And while she didn't have her glasses on, she could see he was dressed in jeans and a button-down plaid shirt that was half open. What a sight to awaken to—fine ass man with sexy accent and hot breakfast all here for her to devour! This was as good as it gets! Widening her eyes to peer directly into his with the best alluring stare she could muster, Arabella made sure he got her message and finished by saying "Yummmmm-e! What's for breakfast?"

He raised his hands in surrender as if he were being arrested. "Bella, por favor! Please stop, before I climb back into bed and have you for breakfast! Then the eggs will get cold. I hate cold eggs."

"Okay fine! Suit yourself," she huffed out in an overly exaggerated way. Then she stretched, turned over and sat up. His eyes followed the movement of the sheet as it fell from her body and exposed her nakedness. Ignoring her state of undress, she donned a pleasant face and said, "Merry Christmas Alberto. Did you make my favorite bacon and scrambled eggs?"

"Si querida!" He said in a soft tone.

She leaned over to get a piece of bacon from the basket. Just before she captured it, he moved the tray out of reach. Oh bacon...where are you going? She watched as he deposited the tray on the dresser, turned and came to sit down next to where she was on the bed.

In the same soft tone he'd addressed her by earlier, he gave her a hungry look and said "I guess today I'm gonna learn how to eat cold eggs!"

That was the last thing Arabella heard before his lips captured hers and she forgot all about bacon or eggs. She gone from being a nerd to seductress in less than a minute. He undid her control with just one kiss and she repaid him by stripping him out of ever vestige of clothing that might block her access to the object of her desire—being skin-to-skin with Alberto!

They made love in a feverish way, like teenagers trying not to get caught. This was Christmas after all—a time to show the people in your life how much you love them—and she loved this man with all her heart. He was her Christmas present and she was his. Her life in this moment was spectacular, bright and alive! She wouldn't regret holding onto it and him with all her might.

******

A while later, as Arabella munched on her favorite food—bacon, and those unfortunately cold eggs, she looked over to the man of her dreams. He was again dressed and lounging on her king-sized bed. She'd decided to wear her robe so they could make it through the meal without distraction.

"Thank you for making me breakfast, and bringing it to bed. I probably would have spoken my gratitude sooner, but I was interrupted."

He looked up from the plate where he'd been pushing his eggs onto a piece of toast. He cleared his throat and said, "My pleasure querida. I will bring you breakfast in bed every morning as long as making love is included too!"

She smiled. "Deal!" She nodded to his plate. "Maybe though we won't have eggs every day."

He looked up at her from his plate, shrugged and then refocused on building his impromptu sandwich. She noticed him drop the fork onto his napkin, pick up the sandwich, take a bite and swallow. He went from a pensive look to a frown. She watched as he opened the bread, dumped the eggs out, and took another bite. Likely he thought better of eating any more. He looked over to her and shook his head in agreement. "Si, perhaps oatmeal or cold cereal would be better alternatives!"

Her eyes sparkled as she suppressed her amusement. "Yeah definitely!"

He finished his toast and she polished off the rest of the bacon. Then he turned to stare at her and leaned on his arm. She waited not making eye contact, knowing there was something on his mind. Spending so many hours together, she was starting to predict his moods. Finally he spoke.

"As much as I want to stay here with you, I have to leave soon to get showered and help Mama set up the house for Christmas dinner. She said be home by noon and ready to work."

Arabella hid her disappointment. She didn't get to monopolize all his time, especially not on Christmas. "Okay. You seem like your thoughts are many miles away. I'm sure there is much to do so everything is perfect."

"Si. Thanksgiving was a feast for just the two of us with little decor and no visitors. Christmas includes all of it. Decorated trees and house, lights, spiked punch. And of course relatives from far and wide will come for drinks at 3:30 pm, buffet dinner at 4:30 pm, and no particular time to leave...Mama is a stickler that no detail be left undone!"

"My goodness, is your mom in any shape to do all of that?"

"Mama is only directing us and the kitchen staff this year. The doctor said not to overdo anything after her surgery from a few months back. You probably haven't been up to the main house of late. The preparations started weeks ago. Today, we add in the fresh flowers, and other special touches. Dad will be close at hand too even though Mama's an expert at bossing us around!"

"I love your mother's style. She has to be good at giving orders with so many stubborn male children!"

He laughed. "We were angels in our youth. We still are!"

It was Arabella's turn to laugh. "You're definitely no angel my love, and I don't believe you ever were!"

After a hearty laugh together, Alberto conceded, "You're right. None of us were innocent. We gave the parents a run for their money. And we tested their patience quite often."

"Thank goodness you all grew up!" She was still amused.

"Indeed! Enough about us. What are you going to do until you come over for dinner?"

"I'm just going to lounge around this morning. Then finish wrapping gifts for the name I picked in the Secret Santa exchange. I'll be over for dinner by four as we planned."

"Excellente! I have a surprise for you."

"You picked my name?"

"No, it's something else."

"We promised no gifts Alberto."

"It is not a Christmas gift."

"What is it then? Your mom is making me my own dish of rice pudding?"

"I wish and no! You will have to wait and see your special surprise."

"Yeah, yeah, so you say! Remember I don't like surprises!"

He reached over and gave her a peck on the forehead. "If you don't like it, we'll send it back."

"Okay." She was still not convinced she'd be happy with any surprise, even if it was coming from her lover.

"Anyway, I gotta go before I get yelled at. I promise though to bring you back here tonight and get a head start on breakfast in bed for tomorrow."

"True, you better go now! I don't want your mom mad at me. See you soon." They exchanged a quick kiss on the lips, and he got up from the bed. She watched him put the dishes back on the breakfast tray, and take it out of the room with him. Arabella laid back on her bed pillows. She was content and happy. Let the fiesta begin!

******

Arabella walked up the palazzo steps and awkwardly shifted the packages to ring the doorbell. She was dressed in a burgundy pantsuit and matching low heels. She was trying to look festive even though she didn't feel it. It was another holiday and she was again missing being with her brother in California. It wasn't quite seven in the morning back home. In a couple more hours, she'd step away from these festivities and call to wish Alejandro a proper Merry Christmas. She'd sent his gift weeks ago to ensure it was there on time. That would have to do. She loved both Alejandro and Alberto. And she was in Spain for the best Christmas ever. California would have to wait.

Why did she say yes to Alberto's invitation to Christmas dinner at Casa Gutiérrez? Did he feel sorry for her because she'd decided not to go home for the holidays? Her conversations with her brother has been strained over these last weeks since they'd run into him on their work trip to California. She knew going home would exacerbate the issue and he would undoubtedly demand her return to the States. Arabella wasn't sure if she'd be going back to California.

She was a basket of nerves as she rang the bell and stood clumsily at the doorstep—wishing she'd given Alberto the gifts for the family exchange earlier this morning before he'd left to help his parents set up for dinner. They'd selected names at a Board meeting weeks ago, and she'd drawn Lacey's. With the Secret Santa exchange, everyone would get gifts on Christmas within a limit of no more than fifty dollars. The Gutiérrez clan had been doing this type of exchange for years and this time they graciously included her even though she wasn't an official member. Lacey was easy to shop for—all things chocolate made Lacey glow with joy!

The front door opened and there was Alberto all cleaned up, dressed in gray slacks and a pale pink dress shirt, open at the collar. Damn he looks good.

"Mi amour, welcome to Casa Gutiérrez for Christmas." He leaned over, kissed her on both cheeks, took all her packages and moved aside to let her in.

"Gracias Senor Gutiérrez, mi amour." She giggled.

"Merry Christmas Sis."

She turned to her left to see her brother walking towards her from the formal living room doorway. She did a double take. If she hadn't just handed the packages to Alberto, she'd have dropped them in a pile to the hardwood floor. Stepping through the doorway to move past Alberto and stand in front of her brother, she said "Alejandro! What are you doing here? When did you arrive? I don't understand."

"I invited him for Christmas." she heard Alberto say from behind. "Surprise!"

She turned around to face Alberto. "What? You invited my brother? You two barely get along."

"That was then. We've declared a truce," her brother said from her other side.

She turned back to look at Alejandro. She was getting dizzy with all the turning and felt like she was in the Twilight Zone. She heard music and chatter in the distance. 'Breathe Bella' she told herself. She turned slightly and backed up so she could see both men—the two most important people in her life. "Are you two being serious?"

Both men smiled at her and said "Yes" in unison.

Bella could tell they were both settled. There was no tension between the two. She'd interrogate them separately later and find out the details. For now, she could enjoy a precious Christmas with her whole life now here in Spain. She cleared her throat. "Wow, this is a surprise! Or more like a Christmas miracle!"

"In that case Sis, can I get my hug now?" Alejandro opened up his arms and Bella took the few steps to jump into his embrace. She gave him her happiest hug ever, clinging to his big bear grip. She'd missed him and was proud of his willingness to come halfway around the world to spend Christmas with her, Alberto and the Gutiérrez clan.

When Alejandro released her, she stepped back quickly wiping away the tear that had escaped her eyes. She looked up at her big brother—her hero. "Thanks so much for coming here."

"There's nowhere else I'd rather be. Now, I'll leave you two for a few minutes alone. See you inside." He turned and disappeared into the living room.

She felt Alberto's presence as he moved closer to her. She turned to look up at him—the love of her life. She was so moved by his thoughtfulness.

"Do you want to send your surprise back?"

"You know I don't. Thanks for inviting Alejandro and creating a truce! I love you even more today for your generosity and knowing the difference having him here would make."

"You're welcome querida. When you said let's not exchange gifts, and I agreed, I figured I'd find other ways to show my love and adoration for you. Other than breakfast that is."

She knew he was alluding to this morning's tryst, and she immediately blushed. "Very creative!" She stretched up on her heels and kissed him. He deepened their kiss and gently pushed her back against the wall. She wove her arms around his neck, and clung to him for dear life with no care who might see them.

The doorbell rang and he stopped kissing her. "Hold that thought," he said as he left her side. She moved off the wall and worked hard to catch her breath.

"Hey Cuz," she heard Alberto say as he hugged the man at the door. Another cousin? There had to be hundreds of them. She'd never met this relative.

"Hey workaholic! They let you leave the groves?"

"Haha funny man. Give me a hug stranger?"

They hugged in a purely brute way. As they separated, this stranger looked over at her. "And who is this beautiful senorita?"

Alberto turned toward her and caught her hand into his. "This is my love, Dr. Arabella Gomez. Back away, she's off limits. Arabella, this is my cousin Marcos. He lives in Malta."

She giggled watching the two cousins. "Nice to meet you Marcos! Call me Arabella."

"Ah, the pleasure is all mine, Senorita Arabella," he said as he lifted her free hand to his lips. Before he could make good on his greeting, Alberto lifted her hand from his cousin's.

"Marcos, let's not get carried away. I'd hate to flatten you on Christmas. Mama would be angry."

"Can't be mad at a man for trying to be a gentleman. Please forgive Alberto at thwarting my efforts."

Arabella giggled even more. Men and their testosterone!

"Marcos, everyone is in the living room. Please excuse Arabella and myself? We were in the middle of a conversation when you rang."

"I can take a hint. I'll see you two shortly." And just like that Marcos disappeared into the other room.

"Alberto, that was rude!"

He leaned in and whispered in her ear. "I don't care. He interrupted our moment. I want you so much. And we can't escape right now."

"I know. But you promised me later, right? We can wait a few hours! Challenge is good!"

He leaned his forehead to hers. "Si querida! Making wild, passionate love to you later is a guarantee. It is definitely a challenge to not take you to my room this minute where no one can interrupt. I'd strip you and be inside you within seconds!"

She grinned and ignored his attempt to entice her more. "No, no. We'll wait until I'm free to scream out with pleasure. Plus, I don't want to leave my brother helpless to your bombshell cousins and their feminine whiles!"

He laughed. "You are a vixen. I love you! And to your point of watching over your brother—that is a very real concern. Some of them are quite taken with American men."

She laughed! "Then we better go chaperone right away!"

"Come! Let's go enjoy the party and all my crazy cousins." He intertwined his fingers with hers and led them toward the music and laughter.

******

The order of things was totally thrown out the window for Christmas dinner. The traditional family table was not big enough for everyone who might stop by. So the family improvised with flair. In the back of the house, a huge tent was erected for a buffet meal. It was enclosed and heated, and also provided enough seating for sixty. There were two lit Christmas trees, chandelier lights, wood flooring, food tables and in the corner, even a setup for music. Except for the see-through flaps that overlooked sunset against the olive groves, the scene mirrored any large banquet room. Oh and there was a fire pit outside that Alberto said is meant to roast s'mores later tonight.

Alberto's parents, or Mama and Papa as they insisted she call them, sat at the head of the table as a pair. Immediately to Mama's right sat Alejandro—the guest of honor from America. Across from them next to Papa, sat Alberto, then she was next to Alberto. Olivia was seated next to her and then Javier. On the side of Alejandro, it just so happened sat Juan Carlos and then Lacey. The rest of the children and cousins filled in randomly at the main table. This seems so peculiar, Arabella thought to herself. Alberto said his mother would never have allowed this at her formal table where she dictated the seating order on most occasions. It was awesome that her sister friends, Olivia and Lacey were near her. Meaning they could giggle during dinner and participate in casual chatter on subjects such as fashion, hairstyles, and travel. She liked practicing with them those womanly conversations versus the traditional intellectual and scientific work ones.

Arabella gazed over to her brother and smiled. He was engrossed in a conversation with Mrs. Gutiérrez. Oops, Mama! Likely she was assessing his personality so she could play cupid later. Alejandro seemed kind of chummy with Alberto's parents. A little too laid back to just have arrived this morning. When had he come to Jaén? Where was he staying? She'd get all the details later when she cornered him or Alberto alone. For now, he'd be the guest of honor—the one everyone questioned. Arabella probably should have warned him sooner about the fiestas here at the palazzo. However, he'd surprised her with his appearance in Spain, by showing up to dine with her workplace family. Tonight might end with a bunch of cousins fighting to dance with and seduce her brother. No big deal! My big brother can take care of himself!

Truth be told, Arabella admitted she was happy. Alberto was such a wonderful gift to her life. He knew Alejandro's presence here at Christmas would send her over the moon. She'd make sure to show her appreciation later tonight when they were alone. This was becoming the best Christmas—one of love and family! The clank of silver on glass got her attention. Papa was asking everyone to be quiet.

"Buenas, mi familia!" He started out in Spanish. Then strangely enough he switched to English. "Welcome family and friends to Casa Gutiérrez for this most special occasion! For the benefit of our new guests and to score brownie points with my wife, I will speak in English."

Mama squeezed his hand and he looked over to her. Such a cute couple after all these years. He continued on…

"Mama and I were thinking how grateful we are to have a close family and friends with us this Christmas. New friends—our dear Dr. Arabella and Senor Alejandro from the United States—you humble us with your presence! Family and friends we haven't seen since last year, welcome home! Our harvest of olives is expected to be plentiful. So here we are to enjoy our blessings. There are many who are not as fortunate as we are, nor do they have enough to share with everyone. It is Christmas, por favor. So instead of giving each of you a gift from us as we usually do, we decided to donate one hundred Euro to causes that are special to you. On each envelope at the gift table, you will find your name. Inside is a check that simply requires you to fill in the name of the charity and we will send forward tomorrow. Let us be grateful we are together once more to share love, eat well and be familia! Cheers!"

Papa held up a glass and everyone else held up theirs and yelled, "Cheers!" And then their cousin, Padre Antonio, stood at the buffet and said grace to bless the meal.

Dinner was delicious…too much food and wine. The buffet table was overflowing with every kind of meat, bread, fruit and vegetable. Most of dinner, the large group made small talk as classical music played in the background. Dessert, round one, would be served shortly. Arabella was stuffed and unsure if she could eat even one more bit of food. Well she had saved a little room for Mama's celebrated rice pudding. She said yes to the rice pudding when the wait staff had asked what she wanted. Everyone around her ordered the same dish. There was never enough of the rice pudding to last. You snooze, you lose. This time she was winning!

The covered dishes were placed in front of them. Just as she was about the lift hers, Papa clanked the glass again to get everyone's attention. "Excuse me everyone. My son Alberto wants to speak. If you will halt devouring dessert un momento. Alberto?"

Arabella was at a loss for what Alberto might say. He'd not mentioned anything about making an announcement to her. Maybe he wanted to share about the harvest. Things were going really well on that front.

"Hola mi familia! I wanted to take a moment and share about what happened to me."

Arabella frowned. What could this be about?

Chapter 29

"Marriage is not a noun; it's a verb. It isn't something you get. It's something you do. It's the way you love your partner every day." ~ Barbara De Angelis

Dinner continued...

Alberto continued, "A few months ago, Dr. Arabella Gomez came to our company to transform how we do our business, improve our quality and save us money. I was reluctant to listen, until I realized she was right. It was time to change some of our traditions, move into the technological era. Arabella is the brains of our company's agricultural future and sustainability. More importantly, I fell in love with her. I am my best self around her. And I want to spend my life with her, have her as my wife and partner. I thought if I said what I believe and how I feel in front of all of you, she would say yes to my proposal.

Arabella was speechless. Her mouth had dropped open and her fingers had gone to her lips as she looked up at Alberto. He was nervous, unsure of himself, a rare occurrence for him. She smiled at him wanting to make it okay. Wow! She never thought he'd make a public announcement or that anyone would ever express such love for her—the plain and boring scientist. What he'd said was so romantic, like watching a love story on television…a love story that was happening to her.

Wait! Had he said spend his life with her and have her as his wife? She shook her head to clear it. Alberto chose that moment to turn and look down to where she was sitting. Then he knelt down in front of her, holding a ring box which she silently watched him open.

"Bella Bella, I love you with all that I am. Will you marry me?"

The silence in the room was deafening. She knew everyone was observing them and she didn't care. There was no one else that mattered except the two of them. She spoke clearly, promising her soul with her words. "Yes I will marry you Alberto!"

Alberto leaned in to kiss her and she almost launched herself off her seat into his arms. As their lips met she instead chose to close her eyes and calmly kiss him back as she basked in this moment. Applause erupted around them. All too fast, he ended their kiss and took the ring from its box—a sapphire surrounded by diamonds. He pushed it into place on her left ring finger. It fit perfectly! Fighting back happy tears she whispered, "You remembered my favorite color!"

He leaned in for her ears only and said, "I remember everything about you and I always will."

"I love you! I believe in us, our partnership and our future together," she answered almost breathlessly.

Clanking of glasses with spoons interrupted their private conversation. It was a request for the couple to kiss again. Alberto took his hands and held her cheeks placing a chaste kiss on her lips. The crowd around them booed. Arabella blushed no longer wanting to be the center of attention.

"Alright everyone, back to the party," she heard Alberto's mom in the background. "We are all overjoyed for my son and darling Arabella! Now let's give the happy couple a break, a little privacy. Please start the music." And just like that the music began again. People turned their attention back to dessert and lively conversations as if there was never an announcement and marriage proposal. Thank goodness for Alberto's mom yet again.

Alberto rose to his feet, and pulled her up gently by the hand. "Thank you for making me the happiest man alive!"

"You're welcome. I had no idea you wanted to marry me."

"I have for a while. I wanted Alejandro to be here and to do it the proper way."

She'd forgotten all about her brother. She turned to look over her shoulder to where he was sitting. Alejandro must have seen her turn. He winked at her with a smile. Then held up his glass in toast. He knew about this! She mouthed a silent "thank you" and turned back to Alberto. "If I didn't love you, I'd kill you for keeping this from me, and enlisting my brother's support."

"Mia culpa querida! I wanted this day to be special. I hoped you'd believe in our love and say yes. I was an ass to you, and then I fell under your seductive love spell. I am now forever held captive against my will!"

"You are silly," she giggled. "I'll get you later."

"Do you promise?"

Before she could answer, they were interrupted by Papa.

"Congrats my son," Papa said as he slapped Alberto's shoulder. "Dearest Arabella thanks for putting our love sick child out of his misery. He's been driving us crazy with details for weeks."

"Thanks Papa." Alberto said.

"Mr. Gutiérrez, I'm sorry everyone went through so much trouble for me."

"Nonsense child. You are a wonderful influence on our passionate, hot-headed son. And please call me Papa."

"Thanks so much, Papa." Arabella said and hugged her future father-in-law.

"I'll leave you two to celebrate."

They both nodded and Papa went back over to where his wife sat. Arabella noticed Mama looked thrilled with life around her. Papa whispered in her ear, and she got up to follow him out of the tent. "I wonder where they're going."

"No you don't. Trust me, my parents are always sneaking off for alone time. My dad is mischievous."

"Really?"

"Yes, you'll see. He and Mama act like they are newlyweds. It's a little weird."

"Well I want to be like that too after all our years go by."

"Forever lovers and friends?"

"Yes!"

"And so it shall be!" And he sealed it with a kiss

Chapter 30

"We hang out, we help one another, we tell one another our worst fears and biggest secrets, and then just like real sisters, we listen and don't judge."
~ Adriana Trigiani, Viola in Reel Life

Arabella heard the knock on her office door. She didn't look up from the computer screen.

"Si Jose?"

"It's not your scrumptious assistant." Upon hearing a female's response and in English, Arabella did then look up. Olivia and Lacey were walking through the entranceway into her office, closing the door behind them. Time to turn her attention from work to her closest friends, and sisters-in-law to be. They must have cajoled Jose into letting it be a surprise. He was usually more efficient than that. She didn't mind in this instance.

"Ladies, happy new year! And to what do I owe the honor of your visit?" She knew they were up to something. They were being a little too jovial and they hadn't called ahead. Was it guilt below the surface, or were they being mischievous?"

"Well since you said yes to Alberto..." Lacey paused to look over to Olivia who was nodding in agreement.

"...We think you need a wedding dress," Olivia said finishing the sentence.

"Yes well there's plenty of time for that," she said distractedly. "I just said yes a couple weeks ago, and the wedding won't take place for three more months." Arabella watched as Lacey and Olivia made eye contact with each other. "What?"

"Three months is not much time unless you pick something off a rack. And even if you do, wedding dresses take time to select. You'll have to try on many if you are going to get the perfect one. Fittings must happen! You don't want to look frumpy on your wedding day, do you?"

Arabella was now very wary. Olivia was rambling. She lowered her glasses to peer at them eye-to-eye. "Ladies, let's be straight. What are you two up to and who sent you to save me?"

Olivia immediately continued. "Nothing, per se. It's just that we heard that Mama, I mean Mrs. Gutiérrez, wants you and Alberto to have a big wedding. She's suggesting you get married at the Cathedral de Jaén. If that is the venue, you should expect it will be a very formal event. To make it happen, she's planning to pull strings to get the Archdiocese to approve. And that means hundreds and hundreds of guests, a dress with long train and veil. You'll have to pick an appropriate dress and now is a good time to kick into high gear."

She pushed her glasses back up onto her nose and hopped to her feet. "Absolutely not! That cathedral is too big and my family is small. Plus, I don't know that many people and I don't want a stuffy wedding. It'd be like a production. That would be too much and make me lament my parents not being there as I walked down the long aisle. I'd be boohoo crying by the time I made it to Alberto." She paused, then had a thought. "Why can't we have it at the family's church, invite a hundred guests, max? Would Mrs. Gutiérrez be disappointed if I said no to her idea? I don't want to upset her. She's been really good to me..." Yes, Arabella knew she was now rambling too.

The women looked at each other again, and this time Lacey spoke. "We thought you might say that, and we have an idea."

"Oh?" She formed a tentative smile and sat back down, steeping her fingers together. "You can get me out of marrying Alberto?"

"No, that would be near impossible! That man is so in love with you it would be pointless to even try. And we don't want to see him in full tyrant mode. No one does!" They all giggled, as everyone knew Alberto on the warpath was something they'd avoid at all costs.

"So..." she said being serious and trying to infer what was actually being implied. Truthfully, Arabella admitted she was drawing a blank.

"We figured you might not want to be the center of attention here in Jaén."

"What are you saying Lacey? We should elope like you and Juan Carlos? I don't think Alberto's mom will go for that. Plus, even if I was onboard with it, I already know

Alberto will not disappoint his mom in that way. There will have to be a wedding!"

Lacey had turned red faced. "Sorry, I don't think we'll ever live down eloping. Anyway, no running away to get hitched for you two. With your role in the company, and Alberto's former position, it would start rumors if you did that—especially so close after Olivia and Javier's nuptials. They'd speculate you might be pregnant. Mama would have a fit!"

"Get to the idea Lacey!" Olivia said cutting her off.

"Right! What if you and Alberto got married in Granada? You've talked about how much you love it there. It's less than an hour away and wouldn't cause any issue for those attending from Jaén. Also, the airport would allow international travelers easy access. People you know, your brother and friends from California."

Arabella liked the suggestion. "I never thought about that possibility. Granada's a beautiful city. It's quaint and charming. Alberto and I love being there together too."

"You two went there together?"

"Yes a couple times for dinner and one rainy day to be tourists and explore the Alahambra."

"How romantic!" Olivia chimed in. "That will make it even more apropos to have your wedding there. Mama won't refuse you getting married in your 'special place.'"

"Okay, I'll discuss it with Alberto. For sure, I'm definitely not getting railroaded into being married in the

Cathedral de Jaén. Nor the Cathedral de Granada. No cathedrals!"

"Great! How's tomorrow look for going to Granada to look at dresses?"

"Back to that again? You two shopaholics want me to spend my Saturday looking for dresses in Granada? What about work?" She huffed already knowing it was a done deal.

"Yes we do! Work can wait! Remember the sooner you convince Mama you've found your wedding locale and dress, the sooner you can rest easy not getting married in a cathedral with a fifty foot train meant for a princess. You know, avoid lots of hoopla and such!"

"Since you put it like that, I'm sold. Yes, I'll go. We can look at venues after dress shopping to kill two birds at once. Tomorrow, 9:00 am?"

"Yes, that's perfect. Olivia and I will swing by and pick you up from the carriage house."

"Maybe our men can come meet us for dinner and dancing." Olivia contributed.

Both Arabella and Lacey looked at their friend. Arabella said, "Hopeless..."

Lacey finished the statement, "...Romantic!"

All three ladies giggled.

"Thanks my sisters for saving me. I do want to marry Alberto and I might as well firm up some details. But not now. For this moment, I need to get back to work!"

Olivia and Lacey took her not so subtle hint. "We'll leave you now to your paperwork! See you tomorrow."

Chapter 31

"A friend is someone who dances with you in the sunlight, and walks with you in the shadows."
~ Author Unknown

True to her word, Saturday morning at 8:59, Lacey pulled up outside the cottage. Arabella had been up for a couple hours since pushing Alberto out of the bed to do yoga together. She'd taken a shower, dressed and gave him a goodbye kiss.

Last night over dinner, she'd shared the church news and he was none to thrilled with Mama's big wedding plan either. Their young people's plan was now hatched. The women folk would have a quick breakfast and then look for dresses. The men would come scoop them up about three and each couple would go their separate ways. She and Alberto would have tapas, meander into the smaller churches and pick one before the day ended. No one was to tell Mama or Papa until the locale was secured. She wanted to select a church near the Alahambra—the magical place where they'd spent that rainy day; the place where she'd admitted to herself she was in love with him. It wasn't possible to marry in the Alahambra's on-site chapel as it was still closed for renovation. It really didn't matter to her which small church they exchanged vows. Soon enough they'd be married and would begin their partnership together as husband and wife. You're happy, she thought closing the front door and half skipping to the car.

"Good morning," she said as she got in the front seat next to Lacey. Both Olivia and Lacey chimed in with the same greeting.

Half turning in her seat she said, "I talked with Alberto and he's on board with getting married in a smaller church and especially the idea of having the ceremony in Granada. Olivia, you'd be happy to know he thinks it quite romantic to marry his love in the town where we played in the rain!"

"Yes!" Olivia said clapping her hands together. "This is wonderful news. At least one of you is a romantic! Super powers activated!" All three women giggled knowing Alberto as a romantic was not a sentiment anyone would make the mistake of attributing to him!

"Yeah, I wouldn't go too far proving that about Alberto. Don't tell him I even hinted at the idea he is romantic. It would ruin his 'Mister Tough Guy' persona!"

"Right!" Olivia said mockingly scolding herself.

"I have a box of chocolates in the backseat in case we need inspiration! I'm sure at some point, you'll need it Arabella. Or at least I will." Lacey was always consumed with all things chocolate. Arabella had gotten used to it and enjoyed the international chocolate tastes that Lacey found to be more exquisite than a glass of fine wine. Arabella wasn't quite as enamored with chocolate that she'd given up drinking wine, but that was to be expected. After all, she'd grown up in wine country and there was no substitute for the essence that a grape produced."

"Yes, we'll definitely want to have chocolate!"

Not to be outdone, Olivia chimed in, "and I have a list of the top five wedding dress shops."

"Alright Ladies, *'Operation Free Me to Love'* is now underway. We will find the perfect wedding dress and location today! When everything is finalized, we'll then break the news to Alberto's parents and be done with it. No spilling the beans. We all agree?"

Lacey and Olivia said in unison, "Agreed."

"Excellent! Granada, here we come!" And off they went.

******

The ladies were consumed with shopping for hours. Arabella was exhausted but enjoying the fun of being "girly," eating chocolates and chatting as she paraded around in different bridal gowns. None had been quite right yet. She hadn't minded getting dressed and undressed over and over. The attendants had been happy to help her in and out of the many she'd tried on. Who knew being in love would make going shopping fun?

Her phone started ringing when she was on her way out of the dressing room. They were in the last of the five wedding boutiques. That ringtone was Alberto's. Had they expended their allotted time? She better answer as he was driving to meet them. She did an about face, and went back for the phone paying little attention to the fact she was in a frilly wedding dress. This was the last dress for today. She pressed the on button, and began to walk again.

"Bella Bella, you all done shopping yet?"

"Hey you," she said pausing to listen to his sexy accent. Then realizing he asked a question, she said, "repeat please?" She needed to stop getting carried away by his sinfully rich accent. Focus!

"Where are you? Are you ladies done shopping and ready to rendezvous?"

"Wait, that's three questions! Which one do you really want an answer to?"

"Si, my apologies, querida! Are you all ready to meet us?"

"No, not quite yet. You don't need to apologize. I don't even know what time it is! I'm the one who made us late. I've tried on a multitude of dresses and haven't yet found the right dress."

"You're not late. We got here earlier than planned. Javier and Juan Carlos said I should call because you hate shopping and wouldn't yell at me for interrupting a sisters shopping event!"

"Oh? So your brothers are using you?" Smiling, she already thought she knew his response.

"Pretty much. Not an unusual occurrence."

Arabella laughed out loud at that true statement and began walking again towards the square pedestal located in the center of the shoppe. There her friends sat on a divan sipping champagne, eating chocolates and talking to the boutique owner. As she climbed the step, she said to

Alberto, "Tell your brothers I appreciate the vote of confidence and they have to wait! I am trying on one more dress, and I am expecting them to be nice to you because I said so!"

"That's the one," Olivia said holding her hands to her mouth. "You look exquisite!"

Seeing and hearing Olivia in spite of holding the phone, she lifted her skirt, stepped up onto the dais and slowly turned to look in the mirror. There she saw the image of beauty staring back at her. Wow, she loved this dress! It had a bodice with a straight line, floor length skirt, and layers of tulle in a floral overlay that made her look like a dainty angel.

"Bella, you still there?" Alberto said on the other end of the line. She'd forgotten they were talking.

"Si, si, sorry. I was distracted. I think I found my wedding dress!" She was mesmerized by its beauty and elegance.

"That's good. You can't get married naked, not that I'd mind if you did."

"Uuhhuh...Okay, I have to go. We'll meet you all in the main square in forty-five minutes. I love you." She clicked off the phone not waiting for his response.

"Was that our men calling?" Lacey said giggling as she popped another chocolate in her mouth.

"You know it was," said Olivia. "I bet they put Alberto up to it. They are so impatient when we go shopping. We've not even exceeded our time."

Arabella was half listening to them as the seamstress made the necessary nips and tucks on the dress. Could she do this? Walk down the aisle with a church full of people watching? Attending a work event for charity was one thing, but being the main attraction for so many hours was something totally different. What if I fall going down the aisle?

"You won't. Your brother will not let that happen."

"Did I say that aloud?" Arabella turned her head to her friends.

"Yes dear. Stop worrying! You will be the most beautiful bride Granada has ever married off to her beloved!"

"I don't always agree with romance novelist Olivia here." Lacey paused. "This time though, I am in one hundred percent concurrence. You, wearing that dress, will knock the wind from your arrogant fiancé's chest. The more important question is, will he faint upon seeing your vision of beauty?"

They all laughed at that statement. With each moment, Arabella's nerves were calming. She was going to marry her dream love, Alberto, even if she had to fall down before she got to the altar. She'd pick herself up and continue her journey as if nothing had ever happened.

The shoppe owner was very pleased to outfit a bride for a Gutiérrez wedding, saying over and over it would be the event of the season. Arabella finished her purchases and set up her future dates for fittings. The group then scurried off to meet Alberto, Juan Carlos and Javier in Granada's town center before their time was expended.

Chapter 32

"How important it is for us to recognize and celebrate our heroes and she-roes!" ~ Maya Angelou

"Mama, Papa, may I talk to you?" Alberto said walking into the sunroom the morning after his and Arabella's previous day's mission to find the wedding venue in Granada. They'd made their selection and it was time to inform his parents. He dreaded doing something that might upset them, especially Mama. She'd always been a huge support and he didn't want that to change now that he'd chosen Arabella to be his wife. He wanted them to all remain a close knit family forever.

Papa set aside his newspaper and Mama closed her book to set it on a nearby table. "Yes mi hijo," Papa said.

"What's wrong?" Mama seemed to always read his mood. "Is Arabella already having second thoughts about marrying into our family?"

He pushed his hand through his hair, and then dug it into the pocket of his jeans. "No, Arabella and I are still getting married. That's why I've come."

"Please tell me you are not planning to elope? I'll never let your brother forget how much that disappointed me."

"Catalina! Por favor, let the man talk!" Whenever Papa addressed Mama in that way using the Spanish version of her name, she got quiet. Her name—Catherine—is also the English version of her mother's name.

Not wanting to be the cause of an argument between his parents, Alberto chimed in. "It's nothing like that. We want to have a public wedding and invite our families, friends and co-workers."

He heard his mother breathe a sigh of relief. Neither parent said a word, so he continued. "We've decided to have our wedding in Granada at the Church of San Pedro and San Pablo. Before you say anything, let me say it has nothing to do with Jaén. Granada is the place Arabella and I feel we connected and were able to forget that we are workers in a company. We love the city square, the Alahambra and walking the cobblestone streets together. Plus, it's close to the airport and Jaén as well; it has good accommodations around town if everyone wants to stay there overnight after the fiesta. So we thought Granada seemed to be the perfect place to have our romantic wedding. Yesterday we finalized our plans and I wanted to advise you both."

"Well, I guess that's okay. It's a small church. I understand why you two fell in love in Granada. But wouldn't you rather have it in the Cathedral de Granada? I'm sure the Bishop would make an exception for our family if we ask."

"No Mama. We like that church. With the reception to be held both inside and outside at Carmen de los Chapiteles. It has beautiful views of the Alahambra. I want to surprise Arabella with wedding photos at the

Alahambra. We also picked the El Ladron de Agua for our wedding night."

"But..."

"Catalina, it is not your wedding. Let the couple have their day where they want!"

Alberto watched Mama and Papa look at each other. "Very good mi hijo. Whatever you and Arabella want," Mama said without looking away from her husband. Papa won that battle.

"Thank you Mama. Papa. You've done so much for us. Arabella and I want everyone to be happy. We also were wondering if you'd manage the guest list and invitations. Will you?"

Mama turned her attention back to stare his way. She smiled and nodded. "I'd love to mi hijo. And please know in spite of my meaningless squabbles with your father, it has nothing to do with you. We are all delighted that you and Arabella will marry here near home. Now come give me a hug?"

He'd done as she'd requested, closing the distance and kneeling down to throw his arms around his amazing mother. When she held him, he'd felt the comfort of mama's touch—all was right with the world in these moments.

Chapter 33

"Live your truth. Express your love. Share your enthusiasm. Take action towards your dreams. Walk your talk. Dance and sing to your music. Embrace your blessings. Make today worth remembering."
~ Steve Maraboli

Three Months Later...

"Well Sis, your wedding day has arrived!"

Arabella looked through the vanity mirror to see her one and only brother approaching from the open doorway. Alejandro was so handsome and debonair in his suit. He looked like a younger version of their dad. "So it has my brother. You look all put together."

"Why aren't you dressed yet?"

Bella looked over at the clock on the armoire. "It's still early. We have two hours until the ceremony and it's just up the hill from here." She was staying at the El Ladron de Agua in the Generalife suite. This was the place they'd escape back to for their wedding night. Alberto rented out the entire hotel for their privacy. This, and the reception location, the Carmen de los Chapiteles—which housed Alejandro, Alberto, and his brothers to dress for the ceremony.

She watched Alejandro look around the room. He was standing directly behind her now and she preferred looking at him from the mirror. He seemed less bossy. "Where are your maids in waiting? There was no one to halt my entrance."

She laughed out knowing he was alluding to her soon to be sisters-in-laws and friends, Lacey and Olivia. "You are so dramatic my dear brother! They're off doing girl stuff I'm sure. We've taken over the entire hotel. Who would they need to protect me from?"

"No one now that you've gone ahead and fallen in love with that scoundrel!"

"Alejandro, stop brooding on my wedding day." She frowned. "I thought you and Alberto made peace?"

"We did!"

"So why the comment?"

"There's no one who's good enough for my sister. But I do think you picked a good mate. And I'll probably always give him a hard time. So you should just get used to it. "

"Well enough grief for today. This is hard enough. I am not into being the center of attention."

"Mom and Dad would have loved to be here. I'm sad Dad won't walk you down the aisle, and Mom won't be crying like she used to at every wedding."

She smiled. "Yes, well life doesn't always turn out as we might hope. I do still have you though, my big brother. If you'd just behave!"

"You will always have me Bella, I promise!

"Well thank goodness! I can continue to count on you to be my rock, just like you're here for me today."

"If this man makes you happy, I'm satisfied. If he disappoints you, I'll kill him!"

"Don't worry. Alberto will never hurt me!"

"He better worship the ground you walk on! You're my only sister. And I love ya to the moon and back!"

"Love ya back and to the moon! Now shoo before you make me cry with all this sentimental talk!"

"Okay Sis, I'll meet you downstairs when it's time to go to the ceremony." He said slightly nodding. She was glad he understood she didn't want to start crying. Not today.

"Yes, and you will be nice to my husband!" she said as he moved across the room.

"Umhm, you're not married yet. Might as well rile him up. Do you think he'd believe you ran away so as not to have to marry him?"

"Don't you dare Alejandro! I mean it! Now out!" She pointed towards the suite door. She knew he was teasing her. She could hear the laughter all the way down the hall. Brothers!

Arabella turned back to the mirror. In a couple short hours, she'd be Mrs. Alberto Gutiérrez. Finally all the hoopla would end and they could create a normal existence. Soon...

Chapter 34

"Two lives, two hearts, joined together in friendship, united forever in love." ~ Author Unknown

They'd arrived at the back of the church and lined up in orderly fashion. She was getting more nervous as the seconds ticked off. Whose idea was it to have such a formal and public wedding? She couldn't assign responsibility to anyone else. She knew this was expected if she was marrying into the famous Gutiérrez clan. She'd refused the suggestion to have all five of Alberto's brothers be groomsmen though. Two was enough and she was definitely going to have her best buddies be here. Speaking of besties, Olivia and Lacey as her matrons of honor were now a demand for her attention.

Lacey said, "Me first?" She leaned in to give Arabella a hug and pronounced, "Knock 'em dead Vixen! And don't forget our reward is lots of chocolate at the reception!" Calling her a vixen was inside joke from the time of the ball.

Lacey moved aside and Olivia hugged her next. "Welcome to our real sisterhood and enjoy this romantic moment. I may want all the firsthand details so I can write about it later!" They all laughed.

The wedding organizer they'd hired walked over and said, "Ladies we have a schedule to keep so please take your positions!"

After the admonishment, both ladies scurried along to join the procession that was disappearing into the main part of the church.

She could see through the glass doors the white runner was just being pulled to the back, and Alberto's little twin cousins, Mariana and Martin, serving as flower girl and ring bearer were starting their auspicious walk to the altar. They were so cute at four years old—perfect friends and mates holding hands and sprinkling the basket full of the peach rose petals onto the carpet from before the doorway as they turned the corner. There were extra petals so they could both drop the flowers because Martin didn't want to hold the "boring" ring pillow when his sister got to do something fun. Someday perhaps she and Alberto would have beautiful babies to grow into mischievous and strong willed preschoolers like these two angel children.

"It's not too late to back out. I can protect you and get us out of here," Alejandro said interrupting her daydream by leaning in to whisper in her ear so no one else could hear.

"Stop it Alejandro," she whispered back as the doors closed and the music switched to the wedding march. She put a big smile on her face and posed for the photographer, who hovered as she stood behind the church's inner doors.

"Okay Sis! I mean, are you sure you're sure?"

She turned to her big brother. She placed her gloved hand on his cheek and shook her head up and down so he'd not mistake her intent to do this from under the short veil that covered her face. "Yes, I've never been surer of anything in my life! I love Alberto and I am going down this aisle now, with or without you!" She turned herself back into position and smoothed down her dress front. The coordinator handed her the bouquet of mixed flowers that had come from the estate's greenhouse. Deep breath. She gently nodded her head to the door attendants signaling she was ready. The doors were opened.

Alejandro offered his elbow and a mischievous smile. "Shall we Sis?"

"Yes!" She wrapped her right hand and arm around his bent elbow and began her slow walk into the center of the doorway and then she proceeded in a slow walk down the aisle. The first thing she saw were rows and rows of people she didn't know. They were all smiling at her. There was only one person she wanted to see—Alberto. The sun rose and set on him and her heart was full for what this day would start in their lives. She knew the closer she got, she'd be able to see him, look into his face, and determine his mood. Was he ready to put up with her for a lifetime? She wasn't sure she'd make the best wife. She wasn't domesticated at all! She wasn't into traditional gender roles nor did she plan to stop being his boss. All she had to offer was her love. Was it enough? She wobbled slightly on the three inch heels.

"Stop thinking so much Bella. You got this," her brother said steadying her with his strong arm.

"Right!" On solid ground again, she tottered along.

As if willing him forward, Arabella looked down the aisle fifty feet and saw Alberto step into view. Their eyes met and he smiled, looking amused. Probably from knowing she hated this pomp and circumstance. His silent stare saying 'it's going to all work out and yes I am going to marry you'—it was confirmation she needn't doubt their future together. If only she'd just hurry this ceremony along, they could get out of here and go on their honeymoon already.

When she'd finally made it to the last row of pews, Alberto stepped forward to stand next to Alejandro. The music promptly ended and the priest said, "Who gives this woman to marry this man?"

"I do," she heard Alejandro say in a commanding voice. She peered up at her brother and smiled. Half-turning he placed the front of her veil to the back, uncovering her face. He placed a simple kiss upon her cheek. She mouthed thank you. He stepped back, bowed slightly and went to light the unity candle on the stand just off to the left side. It was her quiet tribute to honor their parents. Alejandro then took his seat on the first pew where her parents would have sat had they been alive. Very moving, yet she willed the tears not to come and mess up her makeup. She was convinced she would have shed some tears had not Olivia stepped forward to take her bouquet, which she gladly relinquished.

"Alberto please take your bride's hands into yours." He did as asked and she remembered to slow her breathing so as not to hyperventilate. In the background she could still hear the priest talking, even though she was caught up in the feel of Alberto's hands on her. His look burning intensely into her soul. No mistake he wanted to seduce her. Her pulse was quickening and her body was heating up. They are in church for goodness sake! He can't lay you down here. Focus or else you are going to be no good to listen for your cues!

"We are gathered here to join this man with this woman, and to bear witness to their love together as an eternal partnership."

Without delay, the priest continued. "Do you Alberto Marcus Gutiérrez take Arabella Mia Gomez to be your lawfully wedded wife, promising to love and cherish her, through all of life's joys and sadness, to honor her in sickness and health, and to bear together whatever challenges you may face, for as long as you both shall live?"

"I do."

"And do you Arabella Mia Gomez take Alberto Marcus Gutiérrez to be your lawfully wedded husband, promising to love and cherish him, through all of life's joys and sadness, to honor him in sickness and health, and to bear together whatever challenges you may face, for as long as you both shall live?"

"I do."

"May I have the rings?" Juan Carlos stepped up to hand the rings to the officiant. The priest held them up for everyone to see.

"Wedding rings are a symbol of a never ending bond and of the vows you have just given to each other. When you look at the other, may you never forget to honor and keep those vows with all your heart, mind and soul!"

"Alberto, take this ring, place it on Arabella's finger and repeat after me. I give you this ring as a symbol of my love. All that I am and all I will be are yours forevermore." Alberto repeated the words and pushed the band on her left ring finger.

"Arabella, take this ring, place it on Alberto's finger and repeat after me. I give you this ring as a symbol of my love. All that I am and all I will be are yours forevermore." She did as asked and placed the ring on Alberto's left ring finger.

"Alberto and Arabella, by getting married, are choosing to put aside their individual lives and come together as one family. To symbolize this coupling, they will now create a blended sand sculpture to keep in their new home. As we watch them, let us commit to reminding them of this moment anytime they forget."

The music began to play. Alberto took her hand and led them to the right side of the altar. Each of them picked up their separate vases of sand. Hers pink and peach, his tan and brown. They slowly poured the grains of sand into a glass box. When it was complete, they returned back to stand before the priest. The mixture now a kaleidoscope of art.

"Please kneel so I can bless your union." Alberto helped her kneel down and then he lowered himself.

"May God bless your union and bring your family prosperity. May all your prayers be answered and you continuously seek God's counsel. May you honor God and each other every day. May your love rise above all adversity. What God has joined together let no man put asunder. And may your lives be a blessing to others. Amen."

"Please stand." Alberto helped her back onto her feet. "By the power vested in me by the Archbishop of the province of Granada, and by the Spanish government, I hereby pronounce you husband and wife. You may now kiss the bride."

Alberto placed his hands on her hips and pulled her close. Then he leaned in and kissed her on lips. While they listened to the crowd erupt, she kissed him back with all her might. All too soon the kiss ended.

"I now present Mr. and Mrs. Alberto Gutiérrez!"

******

Arabella had fallen in love with Alberto, his family and Spain along the journey. This one man full of passion and loyalty had her stop and consider what it takes to fight for your dreams, stand up for what matters to you, and work hard to have it all. She remembered a quote from an unknown author:

"Sometimes we make love with our eyes. Sometimes we make love with our hands. Sometimes we make love with our bodies. Always we make love with our hearts."

Epilogue

"Love is a symbol of eternity. It wipes out all sense of time, destroying all memory of a beginning and all fear of an end." ~ Madame de Stael

The Gutiérrez family's corporate jet had just touched down, returning her and Alberto from their two week honeymoon in Italy. It had been spectacular traveling through the countryside totally and completely carefree and alive. But she was now back in Spain—her new and forever home with her husband and partner, Alberto. She was so excited and couldn't wait to get to their cottage—part of the sprawling Gutiérrez estate that was full of family and love. It would be just the two of them in the carriage house. Alone at last!

As she went to walk off the plane, unexpectedly Alberto scooped her up into his arms, and carried her down the steps. At the bottom he placed her feet on solid ground and captured her hand in his. Squeezing it she heard him say, "Welcome home, my wife."

"Thank you, my husband," she said as she turned slightly to look around at the surrounding land of the airport whereby the sun was still beaming brightly in the late afternoon—this was the same place she had come not so many months before determined to succeed. She'd fulfilled her mission to implement the new olive extraction process and even more she was grateful to find a new family, inviting friends and more love than she knew how to absorb.

Alberto tugged slightly on her hand and she stepped into his embrace. He leaned in and kissed her right there on the tarmac. She had to admit she'd yet to get used to being married even in the two short weeks since they'd taken their vows. She definitely loved him and she liked going to sleep and waking up together, day after day. She also liked being kissed whenever the mood struck him, and was content to kiss him all day. No surprise he consistently awakened a sizzle deep in her core and at this moment, all she wanted to do was go home and fall into their bed.

Arabella was languishing in the deliciousness of her new life until Alberto abruptly stopped kissing her. Maybe they were getting a little carried away. She huffed a little sigh, unsure how her body could continuously betray her will for control. He gave her another quick kiss on the forehead. Yep, seduction was over. At least for the moment.

"Oh wife, I have one more wedding gift for you. It's a surprise!"

She looked up at him, stretched onto her tippy toes and kissed her husband on the lips again. It was a slow, seductive kiss designed to make him pay attention. Then she whispered, "I don't like surprises husband dear!"

She watched him lift his head, close his eyes and take a breath. It was fun to watch him fight for control just as much as she did.

"I beg to differ my wife. You like my surprises!"

"Well I might like some of your surprises, once I find out what they are." She smiled, immediately remembering back to the Thanksgiving surprise that changed their relationship from tawdry lust to love affair. He was such a gentleman that night. Especially when he took her home and didn't stay, even though he'd told her 'I love you' for the first time. She would have given him anything he wanted that magical night, including her soul. One week later and they went public with their relationship, shocking everyone except Alberto's mother. Now, they were married.

"Well this surprise is an adventure, one to remember for a lifetime!"

"Not sure I like the sound of it!"

He smoothed down her wild curls blowing in the wind. "Bella, Bella, do you trust me?"

"Always!"

"Then come with me into our new life filled with surprises."

"I guess I did sign up for that experiment when I said I do."

He laughed heartily. "You bet you did Doctor!"

"Fine, I will come with you into the next one, and we'll see about the rest!"

She loved when he playfully teased her. There was no formality between them, only mutual respect and admiration—peppered perhaps with a lot of geekiness. They were both scientists after all. Reading journals and published abstracts was the perfect indulgence to occupy them when they weren't making love or discussing work.

"One more request: I have to blindfold you and you can't ask any questions."

"What?" He'd interrupted her musings. "Now you are testing my love, my dear husband!"

"Remember you said you trust me. I promise to behave. I won't have my way with your body until later."

She knew he meant every word. And yet again she couldn't wait for them to be in the privacy of their little cottage. "I'll submit for now."

"I do like the sound of that. Now turn around."

Arabella complied and he blindfolded her with a silk scarf. One of hers she was sure. Once it was securely in place, he led her a short distance to a car. Inside she felt him slide in next to her, buckle her seatbelt and said "Driver, we're ready to go."

The engine started and the car moved. Alberto took both her hands out of her lap where she was fidgeting and wove them between his fingers. What a soothing gesture! She leaned her head on his shoulder. She trusted him with her life. There was nothing she needed to ask or question and she knew he'd never put her in harm's way or chance her safety. Maybe she'd finally learned to relinquish control. Wow, love is miraculous when one finds their soulmate!

She felt the gentle nudge. "Bella Bella, we're here."

She lifted her head, and tried to open her eyes, remembering she was blindfolded. The car had stopped and she must've fallen asleep on the ride. She wondered where they were and how long she'd slept.

"You gonna help me out so I can discover my surprise?"

"Yes, definitely!"

She heard the car door open. He moved from beside her and she felt alone. That didn't last long. She heard the door to her left open up. Then ever so gently Alberto said, "Come with me, querida." He took her hand and helped her out of the vehicle. Then he put his hand around her waist. The door shut behind her. A breeze blew in the chilly springtime air letting her know they were outside. It was awfully quiet, so they probably weren't in the city. Maybe a romantic picnic in the groves?

"Thank you driver. That will be all." She heard Alberto say.

"You're welcome Senor Gutiérrez. Let me know if you need anything else." She thought to herself, how would they get back?

Then another car door closed and the engine came to life. Shortly after she heard the sounds of the car die away. She assumed the vehicle had moved on into the distance.

"My dear wife, just a few more steps to go." She shook her head okay. He moved her along and she was getting more curious by the second. They were definitely not on concreted ground. If he was surprising her with a romantic meal for two, she'd swoon and faint. She felt him turn her into his embrace.

"May I have a kiss?"

"Of course. Would you take off the blindfold?"

"Yes." She felt his lips touch hers and she wove her hands up his chest and around his neck. As they kissed, she felt him untie the scarf. Then he stopped and she could see him lean down to pick up some stuff. As her eyes adjusted, she uttered, "What's that?" He was holding what looked to be blankets.

"Our picnic lunch and some blankets. I thought maybe we could come back to the place where we had Thanksgiving and finish what we started. Just the two of us! That night I wanted you so much. Today you are my wife. Make no mistake, I will have you!"

"Oh husband, I do like your surprises!"

"Come!" He took her hand and they walked forward. It was quiet and undisturbed all around them. No cellist or catering staff. This time it seemed as if they were alone. He led her to the front door of the farmhouse, not the barn. She was about to say something when he spoke once more.

"Welcome to our new place Bella Bella! This is ours now. My parents gave it to us as a wedding gift.

"What? I don't understand. What about the carriage house? Your parents gave it to us as a wedding gift." She was confused, in a happy sort of way.

"Yes that's true too! Now we have two houses, and I hope you will want this one to be our home. The carriage house—our little cottage will always be special. And this is our farmhouse, which is a private place away from all the activity of the palazzo. I had it fully renovated as my gift to you. It is more spacious than the cottage, with four bedrooms, a blue office especially for you, and we have our very own barn!"

She looked up at Alberto, placing her hand over his heart. "Wow, thank you! It's wonderful. Now, I really am home, my love, and I forever will be with you."

Alberto swept her up into his arms and took her through the threshold of their new home, kicking the door closed behind him. Arabella was sure he was going to make good on his promises of later, and she certainly hoped he would.

The End

About the Author:

L. Elaine lives in Maryland, just outside her hometown of Washington, DC. She has three sons, a daughter-in-law, and a granddaughter, whose eyes sparkle each time she gets a new idea!

Almost a decade ago. With coaxing from a dear friend at work, she decided to write her own romance novel to see if she would enjoy crafting beautiful stories of love set in exotic locales. And she does, so she continues to write.

Besides reading and writing, L. Elaine enjoys traveling, teaching, meeting people and tasting food from foreign lands. She considers herself a lifelong learner with lots left to discover! She would love to hear from you so please visit her website.

EXCERPT

from the next book

in the series

Dynasty of Love

The Gutiérrez Family: Book 4

And stay tuned for more love stories from the *Dynasty of Love* series about the Gutiérrez family!

Valentino and Anya's Story...excerpt:

They walked into their apartment, with arms full of the latest in trendy fashions. It had been a fun-filled girls day that included spa, shopping and lunch. Anya had giggled for hours with Angelica like any other female who was hanging out with her bestie! And Cape Town, South Africa was the perfect place to live with every modern amenity anyone could ever want—city, ocean, beach, mountain, and plenty of international ambience.

"I don't know what I'm going to do. I have to work."

"I have my key Angelica, so I'll open the door."

Mid-sentence Angelica said, "Wow!"

Anya looked up from maneuvering to get the key in her purse not sure what had changed her friend's recounting of her latest job fiasco. Facing them were dozens and dozens of flowers in vases that covered every table surface. She dropped her purse and bags.

"Wow," her friend said again as she sauntered over to stand before the nearest bouquet, and sniffed the fragrant aroma. "How dreamy! Who sent you these Anya?"

"How do you know they came for me?"

"You're right," Angelica said looking around. "I don't see a card. And they are definitely yours! I'm not dating anyone. And, might I remind you, you are the one who's been seeing that hot Spanish god-like creature, Valentino, for the last month!"

Anya turned red from head to toe at Angelica's description of him; she was spot on. Valentino Gutiérrez was not a man, he was a deity. "Yes, true, he is scrumptious! I do like new things! Well actually, I like attention!" She puckered her lips to think about it. "Especially from a man!"

Angelica said, "Well I definitely think you have his attention!"

Looking around the room at the colorful display of pink and white roses, she was even getting overwhelmed with what had to be over a hundred stems. Anya blushed. "Oh my! I guess I never expected this. Winning that bet complicated everything."

"What bet, Anya?"

"Bet? Oh....did I say that out loud?" Anya bit her bottom lip as if she had said too much. She bent over and picked up the items she had dropped and placed them on the couch before she lowered herself down next to them.

Not liking the sound of her best friend stalling, Angelica turned her attention away from sniffing the beautiful bouquets to focus in and speak very slowly. "Anya, what bet did you make with Valentino?"

Knowing her friend was going to get to the truth, like a dog searching for its last bone on its deathbed, she conceded. "Okay, fine, I'll tell you! I bet him I could sleep in the same bed with him and not have sex."

"What! You made that bet? Why would you bet him that? Who'd wants to win against him? I would have already slept with him...he's divine!"

Anya sighed..."Yes he is! Too much so. And someone has to maintain some control. I am not a love sick puppy; or at least I wasn't that night." Anya thought to herself, I will never give in to a man over my own self-preservation like mom.

"Wait! Stop the presses, when did you spend the night with him? And why didn't you tell me!"

It was a statement, not a question. Anya and Angelica talked about everything that happened in their lives. Everything! Angelica was a hopeless romantic. Anya was practical! Together they were like ying/yang and no one would ever come between their friendship. This time though, Anya had held back. There was something about Valentino that made her want to keep it simple, not dramatic and complicated. Probably had a lot to do with watching her mom lose herself in men who weren't worth her attention. Anya was impressed with Valentino's ambitious ego and how attracted she was to his take charge attitude. Everything and everyone got taken care of around him. And he was so attentive to her no matter what was going on. For sure he was charming, handsome, and easy-going. Just below the surface, she could sense he knew his power and he chose not to be overbearing with her or others. Plus, he made her laugh. He called her his oasis, the safe place where he could lay his head, not have to think, and find rest. That made her giggle - convinced no place like that existed!

"Hmph hmph," Angelica cleared her throat, bringing Anya back to reality. "I'm waiting Anya Francesca Peters! Spill every detail now or else!"

She sighed. "We slept in the same bed the other night when you worked the night shift. It was kind of an impulse thing. We made the bet over dinner the night before. He was convinced I could not resist the temptation. I said watch me! Nothing happened. We talked for hours, fell asleep next to each other and awoke the next morning. I won!"

She wondered what it would have been like to sleep with him. Lawd, she was tempted. More than once she had wanted to kiss his beautiful lips, touch his broad shoulders and taut muscles, run her fingers down his chest, and follow the trail of hair that she could see under his shirt. And she did not. It was a fun scene to watch. Actually, if she really thought about it, it was frustrating.

He was the perfect gentleman, even when he asked her if she minded him sleeping naked in her bed. She wanted to wipe the smirk off his face as he held back the laugh that she could see twinkling in his eyes with his inquiry. She said 'yes, I mind!' She pointed down to her pajama set, the only respectable sleepwear she owned. 'See I'm not naked, so neither can you be. Not to be outdone, he stood in the middle of her room, stripped down to his boxers and jumped under the covers. Suit yourself, he had said. All she could do was watch. It was a very long night.

"I see what he bet, a la your favorite flowers. So what did you bet if you lost?"

"I asked what he wanted. He said for me to make him breakfast in bed, served naked."

"Oh my! I'm definitely impressed Anya! I know it is just a matter of time before he wears down your resistance. I see how he looks at you, how he caters to your every want. You will give in. And when you do, I want all the details!"

"Gee thanks my friend for believing in me! Anya threw her rolled up socks at Angelica!

"Oh I do! What is it that Kem says in that song: *Love Calls*."

"This isn't love Angelica. Lust yes, not love.

"Yeah okay. Mark my words, there is something special that you too have together. I will see how it plays out, and if I'm right, you are a goner."

Angelica's words scared Anya. Losing oneself to a man never went well. She had no intention of falling in love, no matter how much Valentino or Angelica tried to sway her opinions.

Familia Gutiérrez

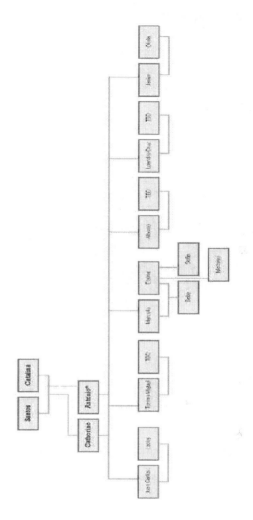

* Antonio came to live with the Gutiérrez family as a runaway teen, and later fell in love with Catherine. He chose to legally change his name to Gutiérrez before they married.

Made in the USA
Lexington, KY
25 October 2019